GRIM REUNION

A shadowed figure stood by a holly tree on the other side of the fence. . . . Jake had thought he was alone in the woods and did not feel much like socializing; but if he didn't, there would be comments that Lacy Honeycutt's nephew was getting uppity from living too long in New York. So Jake smiled and called a friendly greeting just like any good old boy who'd never left home.

Recognition turned the smile into a genuine grin.

"Well, I'll be damned!" he said, passing over his shotgun so he could climb through the barbed wire fence unencumbered. "What are you doing in this neck of the woods?"

The blast of his shotgun took him squarely in the chest. There was no time to feel fear or betrayal or even simple surprise. One minute, Jake Honeycutt was pushing apart the strands of fence wire; the next moment, he lay tangled in the barbs, torn open, his bright blood spilling across the brown pine needles into the sandy soil beneath.

Gloved hands dropped the shotgun beside the body and soon there was only the raucous scream of blue jays and the puzzled whine of the dogs to break the morning's new silence.

By Margaret Maron

BLOODY KIN

Margaret Maron

BANTAM BOOKS
NEW YORK · TORONTO · LONDON · SYDNEY · AUCKLAND

While North Carolina is—happily—much more than a state of mind, it has no county named for Sir John Colleton, one of King Charles II's Lord Proprietors. In rectifying that omission, I should like to make it clear that my Colleton County does not portray a real place and any resemblance between its fictional inhabitants and actual persons is purely coincidental.

*This edition contains the complete text
of the original hardcover edition.*
NOT ONE WORD HAS BEEN OMITTED.

BLOODY KIN

*A Bantam Crime Line Book / published by arrangement with
the author*

PUBLISHING HISTORY
Doubleday edition published 1985
Bantam edition / March 1992

CRIME LINE and the portrayal of a boxed "cl" are trademarks of Bantam Books, a division of Bantam Doubleday Dell Publishing Group, Inc.

Excerpt from Horton Hatches the Egg *by
Dr. Seuss copyright 1940 by Random House.
Reprinted by Permission of Random House.*

ISBN 0-553-29514-4

Published simultaneously in the United States and Canada

Bantam Books are published by Bantam Books, a division of Bantam Doubleday Dell Publishing Group, Inc. Its trademark, consisting of the words "Bantam Books" and the portrayal of a rooster, is Registered in U.S. Patent and Trademark Office and in other countries. Marca Registrada. Bantam Books, 666 Fifth Avenue, New York, New York 10103.

For Agnes Furst Maron, the standard by which all mothers-in-law should be measured

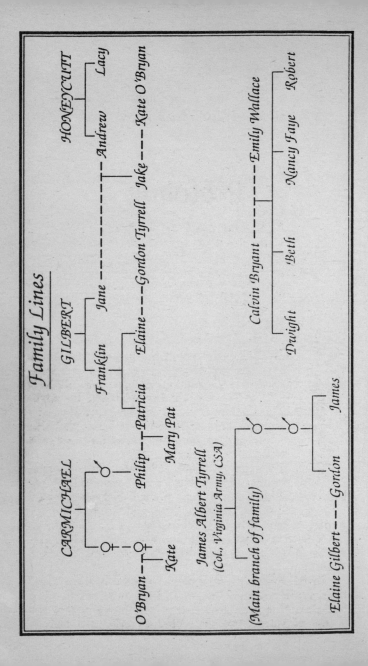

Family Lines

CARMICHAEL   GILBERT   HONEYCUTT

O'Bryan — Kate   Philip — Patricia   Franklin   Jane   Andrew   Lacy

Mary Pat   Elaine — Gordon Tyrrell   Jake — Kate O'Bryan

James Albert Tyrrell
(Col., Virginia Army, CSA)

(Main branch of family)

Elaine Gilbert — Gordon   Gordon   James

Calvin Bryant — Emily Wallace

Dwight   Beth   Nancy Faye   Robert

Prologue

[Second week in October]

Jake Honeycutt spent the last morning of his life rambling through the lanes and back fields of his Colleton County farm. If he'd been told it was his last morning, he might have regretted that he couldn't hold Kate one last time, but he would have been glad that it was ending here in North Carolina, not back in New York.

No one told him, of course, so that October morning he drank a final cup of Lacy's hot black coffee and, since Lacy himself had disappeared somewhere, whistled up the dogs and strode down the sloping hillside with his shotgun across his shoulder to see if he could flush a few mourning doves before taking the 5 P.M. flight from RDU back to New York and Kate.

Drifts of bright yellow sneezeweeds edged the vegetable garden which his uncle kept hoed clean even though nothing still grew except tomatoes and okra and a row of coarse leathery collards. Lacy had already disked under the rest of the garden plot and had sown his turnip patch for the winter. Winters here were mild enough to grow lettuce and spinach in a cold frame, but Lacy didn't hold with such. Collards, turnips, and mustard greens had nourished him for seventy winters and he didn't see the point of changing now.

Beyond the garden were five wooden tobacco barns looking like a row of cardboard half-gallon milk cartons. Their green tar-paper sheathing had ripped and torn away in places. One of these days, thought Jake, he'd find time to dismantle those barns. The boards could be used for something else. Wasteful to let them just rot down. Dangerous, too, probably since the butane gas burners had never been disconnected.

In the old days of mule-drawn drags, rank green tobacco leaves had been brought from the fields and string-tied by the handfuls onto four-foot sticks, about twenty-five bunches to the stick; then hung in the tall barns for heat curing, about eight hundred sticks to the barn. Originally, the furnaces were fired by hardwood cut in the winter, and men who had worked all day in the hot fields priming tobacco slept beside their barns and kept the fires going through the night. After World War II, wood gave way to oil burners with thermostats and later to gas, so that a farmer could sleep in his own bed, though Jake remembered how his father still got up in the middle of the night to check on the barns. A broken stick or a single loose leaf falling on a hot flue could send a barn up in flames and destroy a summer's profits.

After several days of heat, the green leaves would be cured to a mellow gold, rich and fragrant in aroma.

From the barn the sticks of cured tobacco were loaded onto a flatbed and hauled to the packhouse where they were piled in head-high stacks. There, women and children carefully broke the strings and hand-stripped the leaves from the sticks. The soft lemony leaves would be graded by color and size and then bundled for market.

Getting tobacco from plantbed to warehouse used

to be a painstaking, labor-intensive process that lasted well into November or December—"a thirteen-month crop," farmers joked, for plantbeds were often readied in December before the crop was completely sold.

Mechanization changed all that. A tobacco harvester could strip the proper number of leaves from each plant and place them in big wire baskets that were hydraulically maneuvered into bulk containers that looked like tin boxcars and were heated by thermostatically controlled gas burners. No more hand-bundling either. Instead, the loose cured leaves were simply sheeted up in large squares of burlap, two hundred pounds at a time, and most of the crop had been auctioned off by mid-September.

All around the countryside, wooden barns like Jake's were falling into ruin. His own tobacco allotmemt was leased to a nearby farmer who utilized machines and migrants instead of year-round tenants, so it had been at least ten years since these barns were used.

One of the dogs put his cold nose against Jake's hand and looked at him reproachfully.

"Okay," he smiled. "No more daydreaming."

He skirted the barns and walked on down a sloping field given over to sweet potatoes. Although it was the second week in October, the vines continued green and lush because night temperatures had not yet dipped below the mid-fifties.

Even so, summer fought a rearguard action all around him. Morning glories still raised their blue trumpets skyward and oaks and maples had not yet begun to turn; but Virginia creeper wound like scarlet ribbons through the pines, and green sassafras trees at the edge of the woods were mottled orange and yellow.

The dogs found their favorite path through the trees and Jake followed.

These woods had been timbered by his father thirty years earlier. Fair-sized jack oaks, maples, and yellow pines now shaded the old mule lanes, but they were

saplings compared to the huge turpentine pines that
Jake remembered from his boyhood. He had not cried
when those giants crashed to earth and were hauled
away to the sawmill because his father had quietly explained how much money they needed to keep the land
together after the expenses of his mother's last opera-
tion and funeral. Nevertheless, Jake never forgot how
sunlight used to shaft through those tall straight longleaf pines.

In France once, he and Kate had wandered into an
old cathedral early one morning and something about
the way the sun streamed around and through that forest of gray stone columns had made Jake suddenly
homesick for the farm.

The original grant from the Lords Proprietor in the
late 1600s had conveyed to one Andrew Hunicut several thousand acres of central Carolina bottomland. One
hundred and twenty acres of sandy loam and scraggly
woods were all that remained, but they had been held
by Jake's line in unbroken succession.

North Carolina—that "vale of humility between two
mountains of arrogance"—had been settled inland by
dirt farmers and rough artisans, sturdy yeomen who
planted and reaped small holdings with the labor of
their own families. Relatively few owned slaves and
fewer still had amassed the huge fortunes and planta-
tions found in Virginia and South Carolina.

There were no fox hunters riding to hounds in pink
jackets here. Colleton County hunters wore billed caps
with fertilizer or John Deere logos and rode pickup
trucks with dog cages in the back; and they followed
their hounds on foot.

At the edge of the woods, a curtain of vines draped
across the underbrush and Jake paused for a handful of
bronze-colored scuppernongs. The musky sweetness
was like no other grape in the world, and after the first
frosts they would taste even better, like a full-bodied
Madeira.

The farmer who rented from him had harvested the
corn the week before, but soybeans were still standing,
their pods full of beans. Perfect for doves.

Jake stood a moment savoring the stillness. Far away, he heard a distant tractor. From the woods across the field, a jay screamed in the treetops and a squirrel chirred from somewhere behind him. Other birds twittered and small rustlings arose in the hedgerows.

With a wave of his hand, he sent the two pointers casting through the soybeans. They worked the field efficiently, but after twenty minutes, he'd gotten off only one shot at three doves that streaked from cover too far away for accuracy.

Most of the year, Jake reflected, a mourning dove acted like a slightly retarded avian amateur. Her nest was a handful of sticks flung at a tree branch and her flight was a startled fluttery mess. She and her friends spent their days teetering on utility wires or waddling through grain fields like portly matrons at a shopping mall.

But with the opening gunshot of hunting season, a dove's flight became a marvel of grace and precision. When you got to see one, that is, because suddenly all the power lines were bare and nothing stirred in the fields except sparrows and starlings.

Jake didn't mind, and colleagues familiar with his competitive killer instinct on the stock exchange would have been surprised by his complacency; but hunting was only an excuse to walk out alone with the dogs, to fill his lungs with fresh air, his eyes with October greens and golds before heading back to the city's crowded concrete monotones.

He shifted the shotgun to his other shoulder as he and the dogs stepped back into the woods. Beside the path was a neat pile of brush, trimmings left over from the trees Lacy had culled for winter firewood.

They walked up a slight rise and came into an opening that had once been fenced for hogs. A shadowed figure stood by a holly tree on the other side of the fence.

Jake had thought he was alone in the woods and did not feel much like socializing; but if he didn't, there would be comments that Lacy Honeycutt's nephew was getting uppity from living too long in New York. So

Jake smiled and called a friendly greeting just like any good old boy who'd never left home.

Recognition turned the smile into a genuine grin.

"Well, I'll be damned!" he said, passing over his shotgun so he could climb through the barbed wire fence unencumbered. "What are you doing in this neck of the woods?"

The blast of his shotgun took him squarely in the chest. There was no time to feel fear or betrayal or even simple surprise.

One minute, Jake Honeycutt was pushing apart the strands of fence wire; the next moment, he lay tangled in the barbs, torn open, his bright blood spilling across brown pine needles into the sandy soil beneath.

Gloved hands dropped the shotgun beside his body and soon there was only the raucous scream of blue jays and the puzzled whine of the dogs to break the morning's new silence.

Chapter One

Kate Honeycutt stepped into the yard and resisted an impulse to slam the kitchen door.

"I will *not* give him the satisfaction," she
thought angrily, passing under bare-branched
crepe myrtles which lined the path to the old
packhouse.

Lacy had known she was coming, yet Kate
had arrived at the farm just after midnight
last night, cold and exhausted from the long
drive—a drive her obstetrician had disap-
proved of—to find the farmhouse dark and chill with
only a small fire dying in the kitchen stove. (Lacy was
still afraid of the new gas range she and Jake had installed and he never used it until the heat of the
summer.)

As she dumped her suitcase in the front hall, the
old man had appeared at the top of the stairs. "Oh, it's
you," he'd said, and gone back to bed.

Remembering past arrivals—cheerful fires in every
hearth, hot coffee and savory stew bubbling on the old

cookstove, sun-dried linens on their bed—Kate had crawled between musty covers last night, wounded by Lacy's hostility amd unbearably homesick for Jake's lean warmth beside her in the cold bed. "Oh, damn you, Jake Honeycutt!" she cried for the thousandth time in the five months since the accident.

Outside, a dog barked and somewhere across the chilled fields, other dogs answered. Then silence and Kate finally fell asleep.

Daylight had not improved the old farmer's manners. "You having a baby?" he asked, eyeing her thickened waist when she was silhouetted against the morning sunlight.

"Yes," she smiled, thinking that even if he hated her, he must unbend at the thought of Jake's fatherless child. She essayed a mild joke at what the baby was doing to her figure even though she'd barely begun to show. She had been a model when she met Jake and she still moved with a model's grace, pregnant or not.

But Lacy ignored every conversational gambit until Kate finally gave up and carried her breakfast dishes over to the sink.

"I'm going down to the packhouse," she told him. "I want to see if it'll do for a studio."

"Studio?"

That got his attention. His gnarled fingers paused in the lighting of his cigarette.

"Studio," Kate said firmly. "I'm moving down here permanently, Lacy. I can't afford the farm and the New York apartment, too."

"Jake had plenty of money. You gone through it all already?"

"Jake had a good salary," she corrected. "We both did. But we put most of it in the stock market. If the economy keeps recovering, the stocks should rebound, but right now I'd lose too much if I sold them. I'll sell the apartment instead. There's no reason I can't work here as well as in New York."

The old man had shrugged then. "Well, it's your money The roof's tight enough, but the floor's give way in spots. Won't need to worry none about snakes till next month, though."

"Neat," Kate thought ruefully as she skirted the blueberry bushes at the end of the orchard. "In two sentences, he's let me know he thinks remodeling the packhouse impractical, needled me about snakes"—she shivered involuntarily—"and then dismissed it because he's sure I won't last a month here without Jake. Not bad for a farmer who quit school when he was fourteen and never spent a night outside Colleton County."

She walked along the sandy lane that led to the packhouse at the edge of the tobacco field. The old wood structure, its red paint faded to a mellow rose, was half hidden by tall scraggly bushes whose light sweet fragrance perfumed the air. *Lonicera fragrantissima*, a botanist friend in New York had told her. Down here it was called First-Breath-of-Spring because it bloomed in January, no matter what the temperature. That first day she and Jake had strolled around the farm, these unkempt branches and small white blossoms had been coated with ice. This March day, the bushes hummed with wild bees.

She had met Jake four years ago at one of Philip and Patricia Carmichael's penthouse parties in New York. "Honey, you're gonna love my cousin as much as I love yours," Patricia had promised.

Kate was five-foot-ten and Jake was even taller, a loose-knit, lanky, sandy-haired man with lively hazel eyes and a slow southern drawl. When he spoke of his "little piece of land," she thought it was just a quaint expression; because for all his talk about drawing strength from the soil, Jake Honeycutt seemed as much a creature of the city as she.

His drawl had belied a tough competitive spirit which drove him up the corporate ladder. He loved the challenges New York and Wall Street threw at him. And yet, after their wedding, during the holidays and long weekends they spent on the farm, Kate began to understand that Jake *was* tied to the land in some mysterious way.

It wasn't a particularly beautiful region. Colleton County lay on the dividing line between piedmont and coastal plain, so there were no rugged hills, only gently undulating terrain that was sandy loam and easy to work. Agriculture was still the county's main industry: tobacco, sweet potatoes, corn, and soybeans; and much of the land was personally farmed by its owners. There were few absentee landlords using their farms as tax write-offs, but some of Raleigh's overflow was spilling into the county. Creeping suburbanism created new housing developments; clusters of mobile homes appeared on tree-rimmed fields once plowed by long-eared mules; and sons and daughters who left home to work in the Research Triangle often returned to build a house at the edge of the family farm, preferring to commute twenty-five or thirty miles rather than live in town.

Kate, a native of New York's congested, boxed-in streets, was amused to hear those returnees complain about Raleigh, a beautiful city of open vistas, oaks, and azaleas.

"Raleigh's getting too big," they said. "You couldn't pay me to live all crowded up like that."

Nevertheless, she too found herself coming under the land's spell. Walking with Jake through quiet fields and unpaved wooded lanes, she began to notice subtle differences in leaves and twigs, to discover beetles more colorful than ladybugs, weeds more interesting than cultivated roses. Jake bought her books to identify all the insects, butterflies, and wildflowers with which she was filling her sketchbooks; and back in the city, her agent, Gina Melnick, began to sell the new fabric designs as fast as Kate could produce them.

Once when Kate and Jake were at dinner, an enameled television celebrity passed their table wearing a dress fashioned from fabric Kate had designed. Amusing to contrast the chic New York restaurant with the mossy creek bank where those clumps of brilliant red bee balm grew, yet Kate hadn't felt superior to the actress who wore a dress splashed with flowers she'd never seen growing wild because Kate thought she was just as dependent on concrete, neon, and doormen as the actress.

Jake had been her common denominator between city and country, and after that dumb, stupid, senseless accident—

"Why, *why* didn't I come down with him?" she flogged herself again. "Morning sickness, the push to finish the repeats I'd promised Gina, that head cold—such trivial excuses!"

And what if she *had* been here, part of her coolly asked. Even if she'd been out in the woods with him last October, she couldn't have prevented it.

Jake's nonchalance with loaded guns was the only thing they really quarreled about.

"It's your damn machismo!" she would snap.

"Like hell it is! I've been hunting since I was five," he would answer indignantly. "And I didn't get through eighteen months in Nam without knowing how to handle a loaded gun. You think a squirrel's going to sit on its haunches and wait for me to load both barrels every time?"

When Rob Bryant called that Sunday afternoon, Kate's first reaction, before the numbness set in, had been sheer exasperation. She was so angry, she had wanted to beat her fists against Jake's hard chest and scream, "You stupid idiot! You thick-skulled *redneck!* I told you so. Oh God, I *told* you!"

If only he hadn't been so pigheaded. If only she'd nagged him harder, blown her cool.

Kate clasped her hands to keep them from shaking.

"Hey, now, no more of that," she warned herself sternly. "That's what started Gina hinting for you to try her analyst. You shake like that in front of Lacy and he'll cart you off to Dix Hill in a strait jacket."

Jake's uncle thought she was the reason Jake didn't come home to live. Lacy had kept the farm going when Jake's father died while Jake was in high school. Lacy hadn't hung on to his own inheritance, but he had been a good steward for Jake's and he resented her intrusion into their cozy masculine enclave.

"What do I have to do?" Kate had asked Jake. "Why does he treat me like Little Missy from de big house?"

"He's always been scared of beautiful women," Jake had grinned. "Don't worry, Katydid, he'll come around."

"Have a baby," Philip had advised smugly.

Philip Carmichael was Kate's cousin from the wealthy branch of the family and a New Yorker, too, but he and Patricia had produced Mary Pat and suddenly he seemed less an outsider.

Even Lacy had warmed to Philip. Especially since he and Patricia had restored Gilead, the antebellum mansion which had belonged to Patricia's family and which had been falling into ruin near the Honeycutt farm. Lacy thought Jake would have done the same if Kate hadn't kept him in New York.

"As if Jake had Philip's wealth and didn't have to work for a living!" Kate thought indignantly.

Well, she'd worry about Lacy later, she decided. Until the baby came—the baby they'd planned for, but had only begun to suspect when Jake died—until then, she would concentrate solely on the present.

No ice on the First-Breath-of-Spring today. The air was sweet with its fragrance. It was the eighth of March and one of those glorious springlike days which still took Kate by surprise even after four years.

Only yesterday, in New York, she'd had to wait for a garage attendant to shovel the sidewalk before he could get her car out, and the Jersey Turnpike had been treacherous with icy patches. Here in North Carolina, though, it was a day for light sweaters and walking through newly turned fields. Fluffy clouds drifted across clear blue skies and the voice of the tractor was loud in the land.

"I was right," she thought, suddenly relaxing. "Despite all the memories, Gina's forebodings, and Lacy's hostility, I was right to come here."

She held her hands up to the sunlight and was pleased by their steadiness.

The packhouse door stood half ajar and she pulled it open.

The old barnlike building sat on a slight slope. Its large upper room, the striproom, had high exposed rafters. It was spacious and felt dry and airy, even though light entered from only one small window and the open door behind her. The walls and floor were unpainted boards milled from trees Jake's grandfather had cut. Some of the planks were more than fifteen inches wide and still held the mellow aroma of cured tobacco.

This was where those yellow-gold leaves had been stripped from the sticks on which they had been cured, then carefully sorted by size and color and hand-tied into small bundles before being carried to a warehouse over at Dobbs, the county seat, and auctioned to the highest bidder.

A trapdoor at the far side of the striproom led down to the ordering pit, a sort of half-basement with solid brick walls and dirt floor built into the side of the slope. There, another larger door led directly outside so that tobacco could be packed temporarily into the pit immediately from the curing barn if the leaves were too brittle to handle without shattering. In the cool darkness, moisture from the earth had made the dry leaves pliable again.

With the passing of mules, large families, and year-round tenant help, raising tobacco had become unprofitable without a heavy investment in mechanical equipment. Lacy couldn't manage alone so Jake had leased all his crop allotments to a nearby farmer, who trucked the tobacco from the Honeycutt fields to his own modern barns. Curing and readying for market had become a simpler, mechanized process.

The packhouse no longer served tobacco, but Lacy still used the pit to age his apple cider.

Well, she certainly wouldn't interfere with *that*, Kate thought. The ordering pit had always struck her as a perfect snake hole and Lacy was welcome to its damp cobwebby depths.

She stood in the center of the large room, measuring its potential as a studio. Lacy had exaggerated about the floor. True, there seemed to be a rotten spot under the window where rain had seeped in around the casing and one corner of the trapdoor had broken, leaving a hole about the size of an outspread hand, but otherwise the old planks seemed quite sound.

The one window was on the north wall.

"Rip it out and replace the whole wall with glass," Kate thought. "I can set up my drawing table there. Clear out all this rubbish and line that wall with shelves. Maybe a sink over here? Running water lines from the house ought not to be too expensive. Replace that light bulb dangling from the ceiling with fluorescent fixtures . . . wonder if there's a socket for a coffee maker?"

Her blue-green eyes followed the wiring from the light bulb across the ceiling rafters and down the wall to where it disappeared in a dark corner behind a pile of tobacco sticks jumbled onto a bundle of burlap sacks. She tugged at the burlap and several small furry forms skittered across the floor to hide beneath another pile of rubbish.

"Oh, dear Lord! Not rats, too?"

Kate armed herself with a sturdy, four-foot-long tobacco stick. Spiders usually died every fall and snakes at least hibernated from October till April, but rats were a vermin for all seasons. She gingerly poked the burlap.

"Mwrp?"

A big gray Maltese rose and stretched among the burlap folds. The three kittens she'd been nursing when Kate spooked them came scrambling back upon hearing the mother cat's reassuring purr.

"Why, Fluff!" Kate laughed. "You're a mother."

The big farm cat yawned complacently and lifted her head for Kate to stroke her. The kittens were almost exact replicas: the same smoky gray with elegant white bibs and neat white paws. Adorable.

"One uff 'em's mine," a small voice asserted.

Kate whirled. The child who stood just inside the doorway was very young and thin, but sturdily built, with enormous brown eyes and dark curly hair which was caught up in two perky ponytails by red ribbons.

She wore red knit slacks and a rather grubby white pullover and she carried a fourth gray kitten. There was something disturbingly familiar about the tot which Kate couldn't quite put her finger on.

"Well, hello," she smiled. "Did you bring your kitten back to visit its mother?"

"This one's not mine," the child said, placing the new kitten next to Fluff. "All my kitty's feet are *white*." She looked up at Kate anxiously. "Which could my kitty *be*?"

Kate looked at the four kittens tumbling about their mother and was perplexed by their sameness. "But look, sweetheart. All the kittens have white feet."

The little girl shook her head stubbornly. "Not really and truly. They just look like they do. I want *my* kitty. The one Uncle Lacy gave me."

Suddenly, Kate knew who the child was and she was furious with Lacy for not telling her that Gilead had been opened again. She cupped the tiny chin— Philip's chin—in her hand and looked into eyes so like Patricia's. "Don't you remember me, Mary Pat?" she asked softly. "Your father and I were cousins."

"Daddy's dead," the little girl told her.

"I know, sweetheart," Kate said helplessly.

"And Mommy and Aunt 'Laine and Uncle James and Cousin Jake and Cousin Kate." Her voice was quite matter-of-fact.

"No, Mary Pat, *I'm* Kate. You haven't seen me in almost a year, but I'm not dead."

The child looked at her dubiously and pulled away from her touch.

"There's just me and Uncle Gordon and Uncle Lacy that's not dead," she insisted, stroking Fluff's fur.

One of the kittens tumbled off the pile of burlap and danced across the floor. Mary Pat was after it in a flash.

"There he *is!*" she shrieked. "My kitty!"

Before she could grab it, the kitten dived through the hole in the trapdoor and refused to be coaxed out again.

"Wait," said Kate. "I'll open it for you."

She tugged on the rope handle and the door creaked up heavily. The light bulb overhead was so dim that at first Kate thought the dark heap at the foot of the steps was another bundle of burlap.

Then Mary Pat said, "Is he dead, too?"

Chapter
Two

 Robert Bryant couldn't quite keep from grinning as he drove out from Raleigh. An unidentified body discovered less than a thousand feet from his mother's house and she was forced to miss all the initial excitement.

He had no idea how she'd heard about the dead man so quickly this morning, but it never occurred to him to doubt her facts. As principal of Zachary Taylor High School, Emily Bryant kept tabs on the whole community and frustration had filled her voice when she telephoned Rob.

"I can't get hold of Dwight and the county supervisors are due here this morning, so I can't possibly leave before noon," she'd fumed. "But at least you'll be there and you can fill me in."

"Why will I be there?" Rob had asked cautiously.

"You're one of Mary Pat's trustees, aren't you? The child should have someone—"

"I keep telling you, Mother, I'm not her trustee. A bank in New York is trustee and they only delegated me to keep a watching brief. Besides, Gordon's there and he's her legal guardian."

"Well, you were Jake's lawyer, weren't you?" she wheedled. "It's his packhouse and his widow, isn't it? Oh, poor Kate! How dreadful for her." Miss Emily's natural sympathies overtopped her curiosity and, in the end, Rob had agreed to go out and offer his services.

He took his foot off the gas as he neared a neat white frame house that stood on the eastern edge of Gilead, the old Gilbert family plantation.

Philip Carmichael's money had sloshed over it, too, but Rob could remember how shabby the little house was when Patricia and Elaine Gilbert were girls.

He remembered barefoot summers here, lukewarm Kool-Aid and climbing the chinaball trees that shaded the front porch. Elaine was a daredevil even back then, hanging upside down from the highest limbs; at the creek, always swinging out further on the rope than anyone else before splashing down near the rocks; slinging nasties on her father's old Allis-Chalmers tractor during barning time. That was before Franklin Gilbert had stopped trying to make a go of the farm himself.

Even after the girls grew up, Franklin Gilbert had remained in the overseer's cottage, a self-imposed exile and all alone until his gathering senility required a nursing home in Raleigh. Something had gone out of Franklin when he'd had to abandon Gilead and move into a hired man's house. Selling off the last of the good furniture hadn't compensated for sporadic crop failures and mismanagement; and, when Gilead's roof went in a windstorm, so did the Gilbert family. It was a practical move, but to Franklin Gilbert, it was an admission that he was less than the generations which had built and adorned Gilead, and he had never again entered the main house.

The move had taken place when his two daughters were quite young and couldn't have mattered less to Elaine, but Patricia had always mourned the loss. Rob remembered wandering the big ruined house with her.

"This was Great-grandmother's sewing room," she'd say. "Satin and velvet and silk, Robbie! And this was Great-great-aunt Sally's bedroom. She had a canopy bed ruffled with white lace and when Aunt Jane Lattimore came to visit, it was hers and she said it was like lying on a cloud."

Rob hated to think how much that bed had cost Patricia when she finally tracked it down somewhere in Virginia. By that time, of course, money didn't matter because Philip Carmichael had so much. He splashed buckets of it over Gilead with no more thought than if he'd been drawing water from the old open well on the back porch. He paid Franklin three times what the place was worth and counted it a bargain for the glow in Patricia's eyes when Gilead was restored far beyond any earlier glory in time for their wedding.

And yet, for all that, they hadn't actually spent much time at Gilead. Philip's financial interests took him all over the world; and, having married so late in life, he wanted his young wife and later their baby daughter with him wherever he went. After his heart attack in Yokohama, Patricia had brought him back to lie in her family graveyard on a wooded hillside above the creek.

Less than a year later, she had been brought there herself after losing control of the car on Old Stage Road during a sleetstorm.

Under the complicated terms of their wills, Mary Pat passed into the dual guardianship of Elaine and her husband, Gordon Tyrrell. Warmhearted and generous, Elaine had swooped in and carried her little niece off to their Costa Verde camp on the Gulf of Mexico.

Camp was the proper word, too, Rob thought wryly, for Franklin Gilbert had given his younger daughter most of the money from the sale of Gilead and Elaine had embraced the life of a globe-trotting daredevil. She and Gordon were constantly off to new slopes to ski, new mountains to climb, new ways to risk their lives.

In over one hundred and fifty years, Elaine was the first Gilbert whose body did not lie in Gilead's soil.

Ironically, it was to have been only a pleasant autumn cruise without the slightest thought of risk-taking; but of the dozen aboard the yacht when an unexpected squall ripped across the Gulf, only three survivors had been picked up by that fishing boat out of Tampico. A bad concussion and broken jaw kept Gordon Tyrrell unconscious for nearly two weeks in a Mexican hospital. They never found James's body either.

Losing a wife and brother, too, had sobered Gordon completely, thought Rob; made him quieter and less restless. He'd brought Mary Pat back to Gilcad just before Christmas and, in these last few months, devoted himself to giving her a normal secure childhood.

The road dipped to cross Blacksnake Creek, then curved up to higher ground where Gilead's white pillars gleamed through the huge bare-branched oaks, the inheritance of a little girl who'd seen more of death in her short four and a half years than most people see in fifty. More of life, too, thought Rob, if you equated the world with life.

Take Lacy Honeycutt, who'd lived his whole seventy-plus years just across the road and down the lane from Gilead. Too young for the first war, too old for the others, he'd never been further from home than Raleigh; while Mary Pat Carmichael had already built sand-castles along the shores of all seven seas.

Opposite Gilead's drive, a sandy lane cut through the fields. The western part of the Honeycutt farm was a large wooded triangle and the lane—local wits called it Honeycutt Turnpike—connected the paved road past Gilead with a dirt road past Miss Emily's house. Many preferred its bumpy directness to driving nearly a mile around the tip of the triangle, and teenagers had been known to linger at the bottom of the dip on warm moonlit nights.

As Rob topped the lane's crest, he saw the field van of a Raleigh television station, an ambulance, and three patrol cars down by the packhouse. Beside it, his older brother Dwight, one of the county's eight detectives, stood talking to Kate Honeycutt, whose long honey-brown hair gleamed golden under the noon sun. The TV crew was being kept at a distance by a cordoned-off police line.

Everyone looked up at his approach. Dwight motioned him past the line, but Kate seemed not to recognize him until he said, "Hello, Cousin Katie."

She smiled wanly and Rob was shocked to see how much weight she'd lost since Jake's funeral last October. She had always been slender, but now her wrists emerged from her loose shirt with every bone apparent beneath the pale skin. Her blue-green eyes had dark circles under them, and he noticed how her hands shook as she lit a cigarette.

Dwight Bryant was puzzled. "Are we any kin to Mrs. Honeycutt?"

"You're not, just me," Rob grinned at his brother. "Katie and I are fifth cousins twice-removed." He was rewarded by a warmer smile on Kate's bloodless lips.

In a county where everyone's family seemed to have settled in before the Revolution, Kate had felt defensive at first about her late-arriving ancestors. It had taken a long time to understand that when a Southerner asks who your grandparents were, it's not from snobbishness but from a genuine desire to place you. Of course, it never hurts if your forebears held a land grant from a royal Lord Proprietor, but nothing delights a Southerner more than to learn that your great-great-grandfather and his great-grandmother were brother and sister, even if one had been an illiterate dirt farmer and the other the neighborhood whore.

Kinship stitches you into the community fabric and makes you familiar.

Anecdotes about people dead a hundred years were not uncommon and everyone seemed to have the most intricate relationships at their tonguetips. Kate once heard one old lady tell another, "Why sure you know him! Remember my Uncle Rassie? Mama's second-oldest brother? Well, his wife's brother married this boy's granddaddy's sister."

Since Kate's first American ancestors had emigrated from Ireland in the mid-1800s, she was hopelessly out of it. Or so she thought. Then Rob Bryant had seized on her maiden name, O'Bryan, and immediately she was his "little Cousin Katie from up North."

What began as a joke was soon picked up by local genealogists and, six months later, Kate had been amused to overhear someone murmur, "Jake Honeycutt's bride. *You* know: she and Rob Bryant? Their great-granddaddies were first cousins."

Smiling at Rob, Kate realized for the first time how comforting such kinship, even make-believe kinship, could be.

Jake's lawyer was tall and whiplash thin with pointed, almost fox-like features. Sleek russet hair and rakish eyebrows added to his feral look; and when he smiled, small even teeth gleamed whitely. But his eyes were a clear, astonishing green, and Kate was as grateful for his presence as if he really were a protective cousin.

"I didn't realize you and Rob were brothers, Detective Bryant," she said. "Miss Emily always spoke of her son on the Washington police force."

"That's me," said the burly detective. "I decided last winter I'd been in the big city long enough and it was time to come on back home."

Miss Emily often said her children split the genetic deck between them: "Rob and Beth look just like me, and Dwight and Nancy Faye are the spitting image of their daddy."

Kate had never met Calvin Bryant. He'd been killed when his tractor overturned on him years ago while all his children were very young; but having seen Nancy Faye and now Dwight, Kate began to form an idea of Miss Emily's dead husband. Dwight was six or eight years older than Rob, two or three inches taller, and at least thirty pounds heavier with wide shoulders, thick brown hair, and brown eyes. Where Rob seemed to have a reined-in intensity, Dwight appeared easygoing and uncomplicated. It was hard to reconcile Miss Emily's boasts of all the difficult cases her son had solved up in Washington with this country-talking, lazy-looking man.

Nevertheless, reclassified by Rob's claim to kinship, she could sense a relaxing in the detective's formality, a formality she hadn't even realized was there until she felt the subtle shift in her status from suspected outsider to accepted one-of-us.

"Mother called you, I reckon?" he asked Rob.

"She did. And she's going crazy because no one could tell her who's been hurt."

"I'm with her," Dwight Bryant said, "but he doesn't seem to have any ID on him."

A small spare man appeared in the packhouse doorway, delicately brushing cobwebs from his immaculate gray suit. L. V. Pruitt, the county coroner, blinked in the bright March sunlight, nodded to Rob and spoke to Dwight in the hushed tones of a professional funeral director, which he was.

"They're bringing him out now. You'll have to wait for a complete autopsy, but tentatively—*very* tentatively, mind you—I would say a blow on the back of the head and then thrown down the stairs."

"Murder?" asked Kate incredulously.

"Yes, ma'am, I'm afraid so," Pruitt said solemnly.

"Any idea when?" asked the detective.

The little undertaker was reluctant. "Now, Dwight, you know I'm no real pathologist."

"Oh come on, L.V., make a guess," Dwight urged.

"Well, judging from my experience, I'd think no earlier than eight last night and not much past four this morning. We'll know more after they've had a look at him over in Chapel Hill."

The beep of a car horn drew their eyes to the top of the lane and they saw a young woman standing there watching them.

"Who's that?" Kate asked. Before Rob could answer, a bright purple Triumph whipped over the crest

and skidded to a stop beside the girl, who got in after
a momentary pause.

"School's out," Rob murmured. He stepped forward
to meet the iridescent little car, which jounced on
down the lane and pulled up behind Pruitt's sober
black Lincoln.

"You must have rushed those supervisors around on
roller skates," he told his mother.

Emily Bryant thrust oversized, wraparound sun-
glasses into a tangle of brick-red curls, bounced out of
the car, tugged down the tunic of a lavender plaid pantsuit, and said, "Don't be impertinent, Robert. Hello,
Kate. What a dreadful thing for you to come home to!"

She held out her arms and embraced Kate warmly.
"Oh, my dear, how skinny you've gotten! Don't they
feed you in New York? Bessie's making pecan pies
today. You just come home with me for lunch and we'll
start fattening you up again. You, too, Sally," she said
to the fair-haired girl who'd gotten out of the TR and
shyly joined them. "Oh, no, that's right. You have to
find Mary Pat and—Kate! You haven't met Sally yet,
have you? Sally Whitley, Kate Honeycutt. Sally and
Tom are helping out at Gilead while Tom goes to State.
Isn't Gordon lucky to have such a pretty young nursemaid for Mary Pat?"

Dwight and Rob's plump, nosy, gregarious mother
had to be nearing sixty, but her energy was unflagging
and only her shrewd eyes gave away her age. Kate
knew better than to try to speak before Emily Bryant
ran down, so she merely smiled at Sally Whitley and
waited for Miss Emily to pause for breath, something
she showed no signs of doing.

"Oh, Dwight, good! I was so afraid it would be that
Jamison man from the south end of the county and I
don't know him from Adam. Or else that lazy Silas Lee
Jones and why Bo keeps him on—"

There was a sudden stir of movement inside the
packhouse and even Miss Emily fell silent as they all
stepped back from the door to make room for the awkward stretcher that two ambulance attendants were
bringing out. The women had started to turn away

when Dwight said, "I'm sorry, ladies, but I need for you-all to tell me if you've ever seen him before."

He gestured to one of the attendants, who turned back the edge of the covering.

The man appeared to be about forty. His black hair was short and curly and he was clean-shaven. Except for a dark mole the size of a pea on his right cheek, there was nothing remarkable about his features and yet, thought Kate, there was something . . .

"Do you recognize him, Mrs. Honeycutt?" asked Dwight, who was watching her closely.

"I'm not sure," Kate said slowly. "I don't think I ever met him, but I have the feeling I've seen him somewhere."

"Here or in New York?"

Kate shook her head. "I'm sorry, I can't remember."

"Mother? Rob?"

Both shook their heads, too.

"Mrs. Whitley?"

"No, of course not. We've only lived here a few months. Tom's in school most of the time. There hasn't been time to meet hardly anyone and besides—" The girl seemed to hear herself chattering and clamped her tongue.

"I'm sorry," she said stiffly. "I never saw a dead person before."

Sally Whitley looked scared and so very, very young that Kate took pity on her.

"You're probably worried about Mary Pat, too," she said.

Sally Whitley nodded gratefully.

"She's okay. I left her with my husband's uncle. I guess I should have called over to Gilead, but I wasn't thinking clearly."

"That's all right. She loves Mr. Honeycutt. Would follow him around all day long if I'd let her. It's just that, well, Mr. Tyrrell's nice about it, but he does like to have his meals on time and he wants Mary Pat there."

"Now don't you worry. Rob'll give you a ride up to

the house and then drive you and Mary Pat right back to Gilead," said Miss Emily as blithely as if she were arranging a picnic. "And, Rob, tell Lacy that Kate's having lunch with us and see if you can make that stubborn old mule come, too. Dwight?"

The detective shook his head regretfully. "Sorry, Mother, but get Bessie to save me a piece of that pie and I'll stop in later."

His tone was easy, but Kate saw the speculative look in his eyes as he watched Sally Whitley walk away with Rob. Behind him, the ambulance doors clanged shut, and, although the sun shone just as warmly, Kate found herself suddenly shivering.

Chapter
Three

Casual acquaintances were constantly telling Emily Bryant what a jewel she had in Bessie Stewart. "A treasure," they gushed. "A relic of the old days." By which they meant the old pre-civil rights days when everyone, meaning blacks, knew his place and kept to it. The gushers were usually women who had to make do with indifferent help for which they paid premium wages, gave uneasy instructions, and were truly puzzled by the lack of loyalty they commanded.

When Emily Bryant first came to the farm as an inexperienced bride, she found one of her childhood playmates married to her husband's chief tenant. A matron of eight years' standing, Bessie had taken her in hand, taught her the rudiments of keeping house, the secret of feather-light hush puppies, and how to grass tobacco and cotton without chopping up all the tender plants. She had helped deliver Dwight when a hurricane blocked the roads with uprooted trees and downed

power lines, and later showed Miss Emily how to turn
dresses and suits to fit four growing children when hail
destroyed the tobacco two years in a row and money
was nonexistent. After Cal Bryant died, it was Bessie
Stewart who pushed Miss Emily back into teaching,
" 'Cause you never going to be no farmer, I don't care
how long you live on one."

Bessie had her own standards of what was fitting
in a mistress-servant relationship and she needed no
movement, civil or feminist, to define them; but after
all the years together, she still hadn't pounded those
standards into Emily Bryant's fluffy head.

"Now this is really just too bad!" she scolded when
Miss Emily turned up at the back door unannounced,
with Kate in tow, and informed her that Rob was coming for lunch—"dinner" in the country vernacular—as
well.

Bessie Stewart had dark brown eyes and skin the
color of mellow, smoke-darkened oak. She was no taller
than Miss Emily, but her honest salt-and-pepper hair
was pinned into a neat bun on top of her head and she
lacked her employer's plumpness. Nor would she have
been caught dead in the flashy pantsuits Miss Emily
fancied. Day in, day out, she wore neat print dresses
with immaculate white aprons.

Kate, who'd only seen Bessie's perfect treasure side,
tried to leave, but Bessie wouldn't allow it. "I'm not
fussing at you, honey. What we got, you welcomed to
share. But *you!*" She glared at Miss Emily. "Why'd
they make telephones if it wasn't so some people could
let other people know what they planning to do? What
kind of dinner you expect and you don't tell me you're
coming?"

"I'm not very hungry," Kate offered, trying to pour
oil on Bessie's troubled waters.

"And Rob's not fussy either," said Miss Emily. "Just
give us grilled cheese and coffee. Anyhow," she added
indignantly, "how could I tell you we were coming if I
didn't know it myself?"

Bessie snorted. "You knew you were walking out of

that schoolhouse four hours early, didn't you? You called Rob to come, didn't you? While you had that little dialing finger working, you could have called me, couldn't you? I know you, Em'ly Wallace. You always so afraid something's gonna happen you won't see, you don't use good sense. Ever since you in pigtails you be sticking your nose in everybody else's playhouse. One of these days you gonna get that nose cut off! Grilled cheese, huh! And what you laughing at, you sassy fox?" she asked Rob, who'd arrived in the middle of her tirade.

He did look foxlike standing there in the doorway grinning at her with those small white teeth.

Miss Emily held her tongue while Rob charmed Bessie back into good humor. Eventually, Bessie allowed herself to be hugged and coaxed into admitting that there might be a platter of cold fried chicken left over from the day before, and she further relented by letting him set the kitchen table instead of banishing them to the chilly dining room.

An astonishing stream of food issued from the packed refrigerator: deviled eggs, spiced pears, butter beans, potato salad, and bread-and-butter pickles joined the chicken, and a pan of hot biscuits materialized like magic.

"What more would you have done if you'd known we were coming?" Kate marveled.

Completely mollified now, Bessie perched on a stool at a nearby counter with a glass of strong iced tea and demanded a rehash of the morning's events.

Already, Kate had told how she'd found the body to Lacy, to Dwight when he arrived with two patrol deputies, and again to Rob and Miss Emily. Now, feeling a bit like the Ancient Mariner, she told it once more to Bessie and found that each retelling made the horror recede a bit further. Bessie hung on every detail.

"You see? You're every bit as curious as me," Miss Emily said, complacently buttering a third biscuit.

"Maybe so, but you don't see me dropping everything and running over to stick *my* nose in, do you?"

Miss Emily pounced. "Then who's the extra pie for?"

Four pairs of eyes regarded the fragrant evidence cooling on the counter. Bessie tried to bluster it through. "Now, Kate, didn't I use to bring you and Jake a pie whenever you-all came down?"

Remembering those homey gifts, Kate was embarrassed to feel tears sting her eyes. If they were down for just the weekend, she and Jake usually finished off Bessie's pie on the long drive back to New York, a thermos of hot coffee and Kate holding a slice up for him to bite as they drove through the night together. Their own moveable feast.

Kate tried to keep her voice steady. "Yes, Bessie, you always did."

"There now!" Bessie snapped at Miss Emily. "You see what you made me do? Oh, Kate, honey, I'm so sorry."

Miss Emily patted her hand, Bessie bent to cradle Kate's honey-brown head against her soft white apron front, and across the table, Rob helplessly proffered paper napkins, his handkerchief, anything to staunch her tears.

"No, please," Kate said. "Don't apologize, Bessie. It's okay," she gulped. "It hurts to think about Jake, talk about him, to know he's gone forever, but it would hurt even more if we cut him out, pretended he never lived, that there's nothing left of him."

Unconsciously, her hand touched her abdomen and, above her head, Miss Emily's eyes met Bessie's in wordless confirmation.

Suddenly both women were talking at once, urging food on Kate, fussing at Rob for pigging the biscuits, pushing grief aside with talk of the man so mysteriously dead in Kate's packhouse pit until Kate was able to join in again.

Discussing Mary Pat's unemotional reaction to their discovery reminded Kate: "Why is Gordon Tyrrell here with Mary Pat? I thought he intended to stay in Mexico."

"Didn't Lacy tell you?" asked Miss Emily. "Why, he opened Gilead before Christmas."

"Lacy doesn't talk to me any more than he can help," Kate said dryly. "After all this time, he still considers me a damnyankee. I thought I was making progress, but since Jake died . . ." She shrugged thin shoulders.

"Stubborn as a mule and touchy as a hornet," said Bessie, "but you'd think Mary Pat hung the moon the way he treats her."

"Then it's only because she's blood kin," Kate said bitterly.

"I didn't know the Gilberts and Lacy were related," said Rob.

"Just by marriage," said his mother. Absently, her fingers twined in and out of the chain that held her reading glasses around her neck as she sorted through the generations. "Let's see now . . . Patricia Gilbert and Jake Honeycutt were first cousins because Franklin Gilbert and Jake's mother Jane were brother and sister; so Mary Pat and Jake are first cousins once removed, but she's certainly no kin to Lacy."

"That wouldn't stop him," said Kate. "You know Lacy—blood kin to Jake's like blood kin to him."

Bessie patted Kate's shoulder as she poured the younger woman another glass of iced tea. "Never mind, honey, he'll come 'round; you wait and see."

Kate smiled gratefully and changed the subject to less emotional ground. "I still haven't heard why Gordon's back at Gilead. Los Angeles or Mexico or even Vail I could understand, but here? I had the impression that Elaine and Gordon thought this part of the country too dull. Of course, I never knew them very well."

"How could you?" Miss Emily asked tartly. "They were like a pair of hummingbirds the way they darted in and out. Here for breakfast and gone by dinner."

"Well, *he's* settled in to stay now," said Bessie.

Like many large black families of the new South, Bessie's embraced a wide economic spectrum. She was proud of her sons who owned their own small businesses or farms, tending with sophisticated machinery lands which had once required the labor of slaves and sharecroppers; of the granddaughter who taught at Duke; of the nephew who was a chemist out at the Research Triangle. High achievers all and worthy of commendation, but of more personal gratification were the apples that hadn't rolled very far from the tree: the cousins, nieces and nephews who still hired out as domestics or day labor in the county and who could bring her all the local gossip.

Bessie may have stayed at home while Miss Emily went out to work, but her grapevine was just as extensive and she spoke with scornful authority when she asked, "Where else he gonna live like a king on nothing?"

"Oh, but surely money's not a consideration for Gordon," Kate protested.

"And why not?" asked Miss Emily. "The Tyrrells may be a First Family of Virginia, but Gordon's branch was the poor relations—plenty of breeding, but not much money. And what Elaine had from the sale of Gilead was probably all gone in two or three years. Patricia gave them a real big allowance, poor child! She always did feel guilty about Gilead. Remember, Rob?"

Her son nodded.

"She loved Gilead so much that she kept thinking she'd taken advantage of Elaine when she and Philip bought out her share. The allowance probably stopped when she died, but isn't there income from a trust fund or something? How does that work, Rob?"

"Oh no you don't," Rob grinned.

"Now don't go all stuffy and lawyerish on us," Miss Emily wheedled. "It's not gossiping. Patricia's will is on file over at the courthouse for the whole world to read. And Kate has just as much right to know as anybody else. Really, now that I think about it, she has lots of right because Philip Carmichael was *her* cousin. Except for Franklin Gilbert, who's let himself go senile, and honestly! that man's only ten years older than me. He never did have any backbone. Anyhow, except for

Franklin, Kate's probably the only blood kin Mary Pat
has left in the world."

"Am I?" asked Kate, startled. "Well, yes, I suppose
I am. Here, anyway. There's my mother, of course.
She and Philip were first cousins—"

"—so that makes you and Mary Pat second cousins,"
Miss Emily said, keeping her eye on the moving pea.

Curious as she was on the subject and rewarding as
it might be now that Kate had mentioned her, this was
not the time to get sidetracked into a discussion of
Kate's mother, a Ph.D. at some university out in New
Mexico. At the moment, Kate's mother was a trivial
technicality. Kate was of the here and now. "So why
shouldn't she know how things stand?" she asked.

Rob threw up his hands in capitulation, knowing he
would reveal no secrets since, as his mother had already pointed out, both wills were on public record.
They were straightforward instruments, drawn up before
Philip Carmichael's heart attack, and they contained no
surprises.

"When Philip died, the corporation was dissolved,
all his assets liquidated, and everything channeled into
various trusts for Patricia and Mary Pat. I guess he
didn't think she could handle all those interlocking
subdivisions."

"That wasn't it," said Kate, defending her late
cousin against implied chauvinism. "Philip used to
tease Patricia that she could run his affairs with one
hand behind her back if she'd give them half the attention she gave Gilead. She and Jake used to get into the
most complex discussions about crop rotation or farm
support legislation—things that left Philip and me
numb—but he couldn't make her read a balance sheet
or a financial statement on any other part of his holdings; and after Mary Pat was born, he quit trying."

Kate took another of Bessie's buttermilk biscuits.
"Philip was realistic about their age difference, too,"
she told Rob. "He knew Patricia would probably outlive
him and that it was silly to expect she'd turn into a
financial wizard the moment he was gone."

"Everything went into trusts?" asked Miss Emily.

Rob nodded. "They were very flexible, though. Philip worked out the main details, but left it so that Patricia could have changed some of them if she'd wanted. So far as I know, the only thing she did was enlarge the allowance Elaine and Gordon would get if they ever became Mary Pat's guardians."

Miss Emily sighed. "I declare, it just breaks my heart to think about Patricia and Elaine. Both of them with everything to live for and then both of them dying so young!"

Bessie pulled one of the pecan pies closer and began to cut wide wedges. "Long as you're talking so free, Rob, tell me this little thing: if Mr. Gordon'd drowned, too, who'd have Mary Pat now?"

"I'm not sure," said Rob. "The bank would probably establish a household for her until she was old enough to go off to boarding school." He looked at Kate dubiously. "Or would your mother ask for custody?"

"No," said Kate.

There was nothing emphatic about her answer, but it did not invite further questions.

Bessie Stewart and Emily Bryant shared another significant glance. Both had been truly shocked when neither of Kate's parents came east for Jake's funeral and they had puzzled back and forth for a cause. Their grapevines pushed no tendrils farther west than Memphis, though, so the puzzle remained.

"What might happen doesn't matter," Miss Emily said briskly. "The important thing is that Mary Pat still has Gordon and he's crazy about her. I was talking to him last week and he thinks the psychiatrist is making real good progress."

"Psychiatrist?" asked Kate.

Miss Emily's plump round face became solemn under the auburn curls. "She was having bad nightmares, child. And she'd wear a dress one day, then the very next day declare it wasn't hers, that somebody had changed them. Same with her books and toys."

"That must have been what happened today," said

Kate. "Lacy gave her one of Fluff's kittens and Mary Pat brought it back this morning because she said its feet were different. I tried to show her that all the kittens had the same white feet, but she didn't believe me."

"The doctor told Gordon it's because of all the shuffling around she's had to do these last two years. First her daddy died and she came to live at Gilead; then her mother died and she got carted off to Mexico; then her aunt drowned and everything changed again.

"Gordon says that's why he decided to come back here. It's the most permanent home the child's ever had. He and the doctor think that after a while, when the big things in Mary Pat's life start showing some permanency, she'll quit questioning the changeableness of little things."

As she spoke, there was a rap on the kitchen door and Dwight Bryant stuck his head in. "They tell you to save me a piece of pie, Bessie?"

Chapter
Four

Kate had never given much thought to how a murder investigation ought to proceed, but the folksiness of this one disarmed her.

A place at the kitchen table was cleared for Dwight, who tried to keep sticky crumbs of pecan pie off his notes while Bessie and his mother mixed facts and gossip with their answers.

His thick brown hair was neatly brushed, except for an unruly cowlick at the crown of his head. He wore a dark red wool shirt, a black knit tie, black slacks, and a gray wool sports jacket that occasionally swung back to reveal a Smith & Wesson .357, standard issue in the Colleton County Sheriff's Department. The ring finger of his left hand was bare, but the skin was lighter there, as if a wedding band had blocked out the sun until recently. Kate dimly recalled that Miss Emily had changed the subject last summer when Dwight's name came up and she'd retained an impression of marital troubles. Was that why Dwight had decided to "come on back home"?

He was broader than his younger brother, with the muscular build of a professional football player. In reality, Kate was soon told, twenty years earlier and thirty pounds lighter, he had captained Zachary Taylor's basketball team all the way to the state championship.

Bessie was clearly fond of him and not intimidated by his official rank and power. A tour of duty in the army and fifteen years with the Capitol City Police had molded Dwight into a competent law officer, and she would accord him the respect due his professional capacity; but in her mind's eye, he would forever be a hungry, gangling boy with skinned knees and a wicked hook shot that could sink a basketball from any distance four times out of five.

"Did you happen to take that peeled grape you call a car through the turnpike this morning?" Dwight asked his mother.

"No, I didn't and don't you go throwing off on my car. It'll still be running when yours is a rust bucket back of Junior Moore's service station," she said tartly. Every year she sacrificed her TR to the votech automotive repair class, and every year it came back a wilder color than before.

"Eighteen coats of Day-Glo paint's probably all that's holding it together," Dwight chuckled. "I don't suppose either you or Bessie noticed anything odd last night?"

"Dogs were right noisy," Bessie offered. "Willy finally roused hisself up about midnight and went out on the porch and hollered 'em shut."

"Which way were they barking?" Dwight askcd.

For a giddy moment, Kate remembered the Duke of Athens's bell-voiced hounds and expected Bessie to tell him alto or soprano. It was soon apparent though that Dwight meant direction, not timbre.

"I expect you'll have to ask Willy that and he's off working today," said Bessie. "Won't be home till suppertime. All I know, them dogs were out front. Not much moon to see by."

"No point asking me," said Miss Emily when Dwight turned to her. "Once my head touches the pillow it would take the hounds of hell baying in my bathroom to wake me up. Willy's coonhounds never do it."

"They might have been barking at me," said Kate. "I drove in a little after midnight. I heard some dogs then and again when I was falling off to sleep an hour or so later."

"Did you come through the lane?" asked Dwight, and when she nodded, he said, "See anybody? Notice anything odd about the packhouse?"

Kate tried to remember. She had been so tired when she turned into the rutted dirt lane. She hadn't made as early a start as she'd planned and the need for caution on icy northern roads had stretched a ten-hour trip into eleven.

Always before, she and Jake had shared the driving and she was usually dozing in the passenger seat whenever they reached the cutoff. "Wake up, Katydid," he'd say. "We're almost there."

Last night, tiredness had helped block out those earlier homecomings and she hadn't been alert to details. As Bessie said, the moon was still new, a growing sliver in a star-pricked sky that had set while she was still up in Virginia, so it was quite dark beyond her headlights.

Her lights had reflected redly in the eyes of a possum that lumbered back into the pine woods on the right as her car approached, but she remembered nothing else stirring. The packhouse had been only a dark shape on her left as she started up the slight rise, straining to see beyond the leafless branches of the apple orchard.

"I'm afraid I was looking for a light up at the farmhouse instead of noticing the packhouse," she apologized.

"You mean to say Lacy didn't even leave you a light?" fumed Miss Emily. "That man needs his ears pulled for him."

Kate smiled at the vision of little Miss Emily pulling the ears of Jake's tall and crusty uncle.

"You're the one who could do it," said Dwight,

whose cowlick had suffered more than once at his mother's hands.

"Want me to have a talk with him?" asked Rob. "You know, Kate, legally you're not bound to let him stay on there. Jake left you full title."

"Ask him to leave?" Kate was shocked that Rob would even suggest it. "Jake wouldn't have wanted that. Lacy's been there all his life. Where would he go? No, I couldn't do it."

Bessie and Miss Emily agreed. Lacy Honeycutt might be as self-centered as a fice dog with a sandspur in its bottom, but asking him to leave his homeplace wouldn't be fitting.

"All the same, it won't hurt to remind him who's paying the taxes," Rob said.

Kate shook her head. "Please don't. I'll work it out somehow."

"Was he up when you got in last night?" asked Dwight.

"It was completely dark," Kate said slowly, "so I thought he'd already gone to bed; but now that you mention it, when I put on the hall light and he came to the top of the stairs to see who it was, he was dressed. Shirt, overalls, even his work shoes."

Dwight scraped the last morsel of pie from his plate and closed his notebook. "If you're ready to leave, Mrs. Honeycutt, I'll drive you over and speak to Mr. Lacy now."

"Don't be so prissy, Dwight," said his mother. "You taught Jake how to ride a bicycle. You two can call each other by your first names."

"Please do," said Kate. "It's going to be hard to keep saying Detective Bryant when I remember some of the other things Jake said you taught him." There was a ghost of mischief in her smile.

Rob found himself experiencing a slight resurgence of what he used to call baby-brotherism, that frustrated feeling of being the younger tag-along who was always getting left behind and accused of being too little to keep up.

"I'd better head back to Raleigh," he said stiffly. "Unless you'll change your mind about Lacy?"

Kate shook her head again. "It'll be all right." Her hand found his. "Thank you for coming, Rob." She gave Miss Emily and Bessie thank-you hugs and followed Dwight out to his unmarked car.

He held the door for her in awkward courtesy while Bessie and Miss Emily interrupted each other with instructions for Kate to come or call if there were the least little thing either woman could do to help her settle in.

"I'll be home from school tomorrow by four," said Miss Emily.

"And I'll be here or next door at my house all day long," Bessie called.

"They seem real fond of you," said Dwight as he eased the car away from the range of their voices and drove the short distance to the Honeycutt house diagonally across the road a thousand feet.

"They're very sweet," Kate said. Even the death of a mysterious stranger hadn't kept lunch from being cheerful and friendly and very comforting. She would have to be careful not to impose on their kindness.

"Mother says you're going to live down here for good?" His voice turned the statement into a query.

"I don't know about for good. For the time being, anyhow."

"It'll probably be too quiet for a city girl like you."

Was there a hint of bitterness in his tone? Before she could counter with a question of her own, they had pulled into the circular drive and coasted to a stop before the front porch.

Lacy Honeycutt watched their approach from the top step. His eyes squinted against the bright midday sun and there was no smile of welcome on his craggy face.

Chapter
Five

 The Honeycutt house had been built in the early 1870s by Lacy's grandfather from longleaf pines felled along Blacksnake Creek. It began as a utilitarian and unpretentious two-story farm dwelling, four rooms over four with a wide central hall that bisected each floor front to back. Kitchen, sitting room, Sunday parlor, and master bedroom occupied the ground floor and the four bedrooms upstairs slept three sons and four daughters, two spinster aunts, and a widowed grandmother.

The house was fifty years old before it received its first coat of paint, and after Rural Electrification finally came to the community in the 1930s, a new kitchen wing was added to the back and indoor plumbing replaced the hand pump and outhouse.

Sometime during its history a deep, shed-roofed porch had been built across the front and one side. Another porch extended off the kitchen on the lane side of the house.

The tall oaks that shaded the house in summer and allowed warming sunlight through their unleafed branches in winter had been dug out of the woods as four-foot saplings while Lacy and his brother Andrew were still in diapers. Later, when Jane Gilbert crossed the road to become Andrew's bride, she brought rooted slips and cuttings from Gilead's neglected gardens. Thick bushy azaleas softened the foundation with masses of pink, white, and red every spring because of Jake's mother, and irises and daylilies bloomed in their season beneath the dogwoods that lined the half-moon drive.

To think that those vigorous, hardworking generations had dwindled down to one embittered old man, Kate mused as she sat on the porch swing and listened to Dwight Bryant question Lacy about the previous evening.

As if in protest, the baby gave her a soft kick in the side and she touched the place in mute apology. "Okay, little one," she thought. "I won't write off all the Honeycutts just yet."

"I'm telling you, if they was any strangers hanging around I didn't see 'em," Lacy Honeycutt repeated after Dwight tried to nudge his memory a second time. "The dogs would've let me know the minute somebody put foot on this land."

"And they didn't make a peep yesterday?"

"Not like you mean." He dropped his cigarette butt on the ground in front of the steps where he sat, ground it out with a scarred and battered work shoe, and immediately lit another.

Since Jake's accident, Lacy explained, he'd started letting the two pointers range free with Aunt Susie, his old beagle.

"I don't do much hunting no more and it seemed like a shame to keep 'em penned up all the time. Reckon Aunt Susie's taught 'em a few bad habits. They was chasing a rabbit to hell and gone down by the creek. Kept up the cry all afternoon and they was plumb wore out when they come dragging up to the house last night after supper."

"So if somebody *was* hiding in the packhouse, your dogs might have been too busy chasing rabbits to notice."

"Maybe," Lacy conceded.

"And they didn't bark at all last night?"

"I didn't say that. Willy Stewart's dogs carried on right smart. My dogs give answer a couple of times. And they let me know when *she* come."

"You never went out to see what was bothering them?" asked Dwight.

"It won't that sort of barking," said the old man, exasperation in his voice. "Leastways not with my dogs. Can't say about Willy's. They'll bark at grasshoppers. Look here, Dwight Bryant. You been up in Washington so long you don't remember how country dogs act? You know good as me how one kind of bark means one thing and another bark means something else. Did you go out every time one of your dogs yipped?"

Dwight admitted he hadn't. "But that dead man got himself killed in your packhouse sometime between eight last night and four this morning most likely. Now Mrs. Honeycutt says the lights were off but you were still up and dressed when she got in after midnight."

"I was just fixing to go to bed when I heared her car."

"Your bedroom's still on the back, isn't it?" Dwight asked.

Lacy agreed that it was.

"And Mrs. Honeycutt had told you she was coming?"

"For all I knowed, she could've changed her mind."

Neither man glanced in Kate's direction, but she sensed they expected her to speak. She remained silent. What would be gained by telling the detective that she or Jake had always called if their plans changed?

"Just the same," said Dwight, "with it getting late

and all, it'd be natural to take a chair by a back window and wait up awhile to see she got in safe."

Lacy grunted noncommittally.

"So did you see anything at all? A car or somebody with a flashlight?"

"I won't waiting up for *her*," said Lacy. "Just set down to rest a spell, do a little thinking. Won't no lights anywhere in the lane till *she* come."

"And after that?"

"After that I went to bed," Lacy said firmly. "I heared the Wheeler boy coming home on his motorcycle about two o'clock, but anybody else use the lane, I don't know nothing about it."

He fastened the buttons of his faded blue denim work jacket and stood up to indicate that as far as he was concerned the interview was over.

Dwight stood, too.

"If you happen to remember where you might have seen that man before," he told Kate, "I'd appreciate it if you'd give me a call at the sheriff's office."

Lacy took the dangling cigarette from the corner of his mouth and said, "She seen him before? He one of her New York friends?"

He made New York sound like an epithet.

"Not a friend," Kate said sharply. "There was something about that black mole on his cheek—"

"Black mole?"

Lacy's pale blue eyes goggled at them and Dwight said, "That's right—I forgot you weren't down at the packhouse when we brought him out. You only saw him lying with the side of his face against the ground. When we turned him over, Mr. Lacy, there was a pea-size black mole on the right cheek, just below his eye."

"And she thought he looked familiar?" Lacy spluttered. "I reckon he did. I guaran-damn-tee you he looked familiar. You wait right here!"

He hurried up the porch steps and into the house. The sound of table drawers scraping open reached them through the door and Dwight looked questioningly at Kate.

She shrugged. "I have no idea."

In a moment, Lacy returned, hugging a large scrap-book-type picture album to his bony chest. He sat down on a wicker rocker near Kate's swing and rested the album on his knees.

"Now just you looky here," he told Dwight, turning the brittle black pages.

The snapshots were tipped in with black triangular corners, many of which had lost their holding power. Several pictures had come loose entirely and Lacy tucked them between the pages as he searched. Kate remembered leafing through the album with Jake several times after they were just married when she was eager to know everything about his life before they met.

His mother had begun it in the forties by gathering up all the stray family photographs and arranging them in chronological order. The oldest was a badly corroded tintype of an elderly man in full whiskers. There were stiffly posed studio groupings of children in petticoats and high-button shoes. Halfway through the album, brown-toned wedding pictures gave way to shiny Kodak snapshots of Jake as a baby balanced on an enormous mule by a grinning Lacy; Jake as a toddler on Andrew's lap laughing through the steering wheel of a new tractor; Jake in a series of grammar school pictures that ended with a solemn yearbook likeness of a capped and gowned senior clutching his high school diploma.

Jake's mother had identified the earliest sections in tiny white-ink captions. After her death, Andrew had written the dates directly onto the snapshot borders in firm ballpoint script. Later still, Lacy's uneven printing had labeled the pictures: "J. in basic training," "J. in army uniform," "J.'s last leave before Vietnam," "J. and buddies in V."

The printing remained, but that particular page was empty. Only the black corners showed that several spaces had been painstakingly filled at one time.

Lacy fumbled through the loose snapshots and finally went back into the house to turn out the table

drawer. The photographs he sought remained missing.
"They was pictures of Jake and James Tyrrell and a
Bernie-somebody."

"Yes!" exclaimed Kate, now that her memory had
been nudged.

"He had a black mole in the same place you say
that dead man has," said Lacy.

"Didn't he have a beard though?" asked Kate.

For the past half hour, Lacy had talked around
Kate, ignored her presence, and tried to pretend she
didn't exist. Even now, in his excitement, he re-
sponded to Dwight rather than answer her directly.

"That's right. He had a big black beard just like my
granddaddy Avera had, only his was white."

"Can you remember his last name?" asked Dwight.

"Bernie's all I ever heared Jake call him."

"Kate?" If Dwight felt awkward using her name this
first time, he didn't show it.

"It began with a *C*," said Kate, "and I think it was
rather long—like Chesterton or Columbia. Something
like that."

"Vietnam," mused Dwight. "That was where Jake
first met James Tyrrell, wasn't it, and Tyrrell saved his
life?"

"They was on a night patrol," said Lacy. "Jake,
James, this here Bernie, and the one they called Kid,
and some others. The gooks opened fire and they got
cut off from the rest of their company. Everybody on
that patrol got killed 'cepting them four. A sniper had
Jake right between the cross hairs of his gun and James
was off to one side and seen him and got off the first
shot. Took 'em three days to work their way back to
their company and I reckon they had some right touchous
times 'fore they was safe again."

"Touchous" was the word for it all right, thought
Kate. On the whole, Jake had come home from Vietnam unscarred. By the time they met, he had buried
the hellish parts of those eighteen months and seemed
to remember only the camaraderie and the adolescent
horsing around between battles.

Only once, when he woke up sweat-drenched from a terrifying nightmare, did he let her see some of the horror he had endured.

While a violent summer storm sent thunder and lightning crashing across the Manhattan skies, he had shivered in her arms and told of being lost in a featureless jungle, mortar fire all around them, their patrol leader blown into a hundred bloody shreds, the eerie silence when the shelling stopped, the click of the sniper's rifle just before James's own hastily aimed shot tore through the sniper's shoulder, how Bernie and James had pounded that Vietcong soldier into a wet pulp while he looked on numbly and the Kid vomited in the undergrowth, of crouching in a tunnel below a ruined temple with a Cong patrol camped above them all night.

"I know they stayed friends," said Dwight, " 'cause I remember the first time Tyrrell visited down here. I was just out of the army myself and he and Jake and the Gilbert girls and I drove over to Chapel Hill for a basketball game. But what about this Bernie and the Kid?"

Lacy shrugged. "They never come here."

"I didn't know them either," said Kate. "Vietnam was long before I met Jake and he seldom talked about it. I had the impression that they'd been thrown together on that patrol by chance and that they didn't really have much in common. The Kid was a little younger. I think he'd lied about his age to join. And this Bernie might have been something of a criminal. I seem to recall Jake said he was in trouble with the MPs later, drugs or black market."

"The army'll still have his fingerprints handy," said Dwight. "Sure would help if we had a name, though."

"If you can wait until tommorow," said Kate, "I could probably give you one. The movers are due in the morning and I know exactly which carton I put Jake's things in. There was a manila envelope of Vietnam stuff. I'm almost positive there were pictures with names and dates on the back."

Lacy continued to thumb through the loose snapshots among the album pages. "Durned if I can figure out what went with the pictures of them boys. Jake must of sent me five or six."

"Maybe you put them somewhere else," Dwight suggested. "When did you see them last?"

Lacy sat back in the wicker rocker and narrowed his eyes in concentration. "Let's see. It was back right before Christmas. Mary Pat'd come over to bring me a picture she'd drawed of Aunt Susie and a Christmas tree and we got to talking about family and I pulled out the album to show her this here picture of her mammy and daddy when they got married."

He opened to a color miniature of Patricia and Philip Carmichael's wedding portrait—Patricia effervescent in white gauze, Philip gray at the temples and so distinguished in his morning jacket. Their happiness caught Kate off balance and blurred her eyes with momentary mist. She leaned back in the swing and gazed out across the yard to the pecan grove beyond, to watch the wind push small white clouds across the blue sky while Lacy talked.

"She wanted to see the whole book and I remember them Vietnam pictures of Jake and her Uncle James was there because we was looking at 'em when that Whitley girl come to fetch her and Mary Pat made her stay and finish looking at 'em with us. And after they left, I put that album right back in the parlor table drawer and there it stayed till I fetched it out just now. So where the hell are they?" he demanded.

Kate's attention snapped away from the clouds as she realized that Lacy was speaking directly to her for the first time since the interview began.

"You think *I* took them?" she asked. "Even if I'd wanted to, Lacy, when do you think I did it? I went straight to bed last night and you know perfectly well that I haven't been near the parlor today."

"Well, somebody took 'em, cause they're sure not here now," Lacy said truculently.

Chapter
Six

Kate had been aware of the telephone's distant rings for several minutes before she could pull herself up from dreamless depths and make her body move. Still groggy, she stumbled barefoot out to the hall where their single phone sat on a massive black walnut chest.

"Hello?"

"I was beginning to think you must be out plowing the back forty," said Gina Melnick's amused voice.

"No," Kate said, fluffing her brown hair where the pillow had mashed it flat. Sunlight still brightened the west parlor, but she felt disoriented. "What time is it?"

"Ten after four. What's the matter? Don't they have clocks down there?" The agent's voice became worried. "Are you all right?"

"I'm fine. Honest. It's the pregnant lady syndrome. You caught me in the middle of a nap and there's only one phone here, that's what took me so long to answer. How's New York?"

"Just as it was when you left yesterday," Gina said dryly. "Homesick for slush and sleet already?"

Gina had not approved of this move. "It's the farm you should be selling, not your apartment," she'd argued; and Kate soon realized that she had not given up the fight.

"Listen," Gina said now. "I've found somebody who'll rent your apartment for three hundred a month more than your mortgage payments. What do you say?"

"I don't know, Gina."

The immediate money would be useful, but long-distance landlording might be a hassle.

"This guy's as honest as Abe Lincoln," said Gina, reading her mind. "Anyhow, I'll have my lawyer draw up a no-loophole lease and we'll put in that he has to vacate on a month's notice if you change your mind about coming back."

For a moment, Kate pictured the comfortable modern apartment overlooking the Hudson River. It seemed like days instead of only hours since she had left it for this quixotic adventure. Maybe she should forget about making a home for her baby here and go back to the city where she belonged. The moment passed as she remembered how devastated New York made her feel.

The farm might be Jake's but curiously it did not cut at her heart the way the city did. Because it was his turf and not hers, it was now more neutral. Here were no landmarks to rise up and scald her with memories of places where she and Jake had met when they were courting: the theater dates, Sunday afternoons in the museums, or bookstores where she had glanced up from a table of bestsellers, to find him waving lasciviously-titled book jackets.

The apartment was haunted by their lovemaking—Jake sleepy-eyed and tousled or lustily macho. For the last two months, she had slept on the couch, unable to lie in their bed alone night after desolate night.

"Kate? You still there?" asked Gina. "Look, it's not just you I'm thinking about. My friend really does need a place to live. He's desperate."

"Okay," said Kate, warmed by her concern. "I'll call the real estate agent and tell him to give you the keys."

They talked a few minutes longer. Kate did not mention the murder because she knew how it would upset Gina, who avoided Central Park and took the risk of subway muggings in stride, but considered the countryside full of gun-wielding escaped convicts. Let Gina hear one word of murder and that brittle sophisticate was capable of catching the next plane south. Gina Melnick under the same roof with Lacy Honeycutt, even for a weekend, was something Kate preferred not to contemplate, so she talked cheerfully of settling in and promised she would soon be sending Gina designs of stunning beauty and originality.

"As long as you don't start churning out bunnies and horsies and cute little kittycats," Gina warned sardonically.

Mollified at getting her way, she rang off and Kate went out to the kitchen. There was still some cold coffee in the unplugged coffeemaker, but in deference to the baby, she conscientiously drank milk.

There was no sign of Lacy or that he'd planned to do anything about supper, so she found a casserole that she'd left in the freezer last fall and set it on the back of the woodstove to thaw.

She dealt with the real estate agent in New York, then changed the bed linens and unpacked the suitcases she'd been too tired to tackle last night. Someone—Lacy? Bessie?—had cleared the drawers and closets of Jake's country clothes, and she lined the shelves with fresh paper. The windows had been open all afternoon and fifteen minutes with dustcloth and vacuum dealt with the rest of the room's mustiness.

When she went outside to cut a bowl of flowering quince, Kate heard the faraway whine of a chain saw. It sounded as if Lacy was getting a start on next fall's woodpile.

She added daffodils to the quince and paused at the scraggly lilac bush. Winters down here weren't really cold enough for vigorous growth, but the fifty-year-old bush by the kitchen door managed to push out a dozen or so spikes every spring, enough to perfume her bedroom when she carried them inside, but not today. The dark purple panicles were still as tightly closed as a clenched fist. It would take at least another week of warm weather to loosen them.

In the four years that she'd been coming to the farm, Kate had made few changes to the house beyond a new freezer and a gas range for the kitchen. Lacy always treated her with distant formality and Kate reciprocated by playing helpful guest instead of entitled resident. She usually skipped breakfast and tactfully slept in so that Lacy could enjoy Jake's company unimpeded by her presence. After Jake added a new bath off their bedroom on the ground floor, Kate ceded the whole upstairs to Lacy and had seldom ventured up the staircase unless Jake wanted to show her something.

But the movers were coming tomorrow with the few pieces of furniture she had saved from the apartment and space would have to be found for them.

The front parlor was likeliest, Kate decided. It housed a perfectly horrible settee and matching side chair of horsehair and cracked leather, both of which could fuel a bonfire for all she cared. The rosewood Victorian armchair, pine sugar chest, and small, dropleaf lamp stand, part of Jane Gilbert's dowry from Gilead, were worth keeping and the faded chintz couch under the front windows was still comfortable, but the bowfront sideboard with its ugly parti-colored inlays had nothing to recommend it but age.

The settee and chair were not heavy and she tugged them out to the front hall with little effort. The sideboard was unbudgeable.

"What the hell you doing?" demanded Lacy.

Startled, Kate almost dropped the cheap tarnished pole lamp she had dismantled.

"I didn't hear you come in," she said.

"Don't reckon you did with all the mess you're making." He stood with his thumbs hooked in the straps of his overalls and glared at her. "What's the settee doing out in the hall?"

"The movers will be here with my things tomorrow and I've got to put them somewhere," she explained. "This seemed the best place. I didn't think you'd mind. You don't use this room much, do you?"

She knew very well that when Lacy was here alone, he liked to hole up in the kitchen. That old-fashioned room was long enough to accommodate dining table, lounge chair, leather couch and the color television she and Jake had given him for Christmas two years ago. With the wood range for heat, the kitchen was cozy and cheerful all winter. In summer, it was well shaded and open windows on three sides provided cool cross-ventilation.

The front parlor was rarely used, but Lacy continued to glare. "Where're these things going?"

"Out," Kate said bluntly. "They're practically falling apart."

"You ain't throwing away my mammy's settee," warned Lacy. "Her and Pa got that set for a wedding present from her daddy. They've stood right here in this parlor since the day they was bought."

"Then it's time they had a change of scenery," Kate almost snapped. Then she remembered how difficult all these changes must be for the old farmer and she apologized instead.

"I'm sorry, Lacy. I should have asked you first. I really do need this space, but if you want to save them—"

"They can go in my room if they ain't fine enough for your taste," he said. "Less'n you're aiming to throw me out, too?"

Kate gritted her teeth. "I'll help you carry them up," she said tightly.

Together, they maneuvered the settee up the wide stairs into Lacy's bedroom in the back corner of the house.

The only other time she'd ever entered that room was the first day Jake showed her over the house, and she'd forgotten its Spartan bachelor simplicity.

The brass double bed was covered with several

patchwork quilts, no spread. There was a rag rug on the bare boards next to the bed. A painted bedside table held a lamp, an electric clock, an ashtray, and a couple of pill bottles. Against the opposite wall, between the side windows, was a tall five-drawer dresser and mirror. On top of the dresser lay an opened carton of cigarettes, a worn comb and brush set, a Bible, and a triple-fold picture frame.

The central photograph was a hand-tinted portrait of Lacy's mother and father. The right section held a picture of his brother Andrew and Andrew's wife Jane; the left was an enlarged snapshot of Jake as he sat on the top step of the front porch with the dogs nuzzling his hands.

A straight-back wooden chair by the rear windows completed the furnishings.

The room felt chilly and the air was stale, as if it had been breathed in and out for months on end until nothing was left, only a faint smell of dry flesh, cigarette ash, and sun-faded net curtains over sealed windows.

Lacy seemed uncomfortable with Kate in his room and gave her no time to sightsee. As soon as they had placed the settee next to the chair, he held the door for her to leave.

He carried up the banished chair and lamp alone without comment, but balked again when Kate told him the sideboard had to go, too.

"That come from Gilead," he protested.

So Kate knew.

Patricia had tried to wheedle Jake out of the sugar chest and lamp stand while she was restoring Gilead, but when Kate later offered to return the sideboard, Patricia had refused in mock horror.

"All Gilead's geese weren't swans, honey," she'd giggled, "and that thing's a real turkey."

"It's too heavy to carry upstairs," said Kate, "but maybe we could slide it out to the hall and I'll get the movers to do something with it tomorrow."

Despite his age, Lacy was still strong, yet even with

Kate's help, the solid oak hulk resisted mightily. The floor beneath shrieked as they managed to heave it a few inches away from the wall.

"Can I help?" asked a pleasant masculine voice.

Kate straightened to see a vaguely familiar man standing outside the parlor door. Just under six feet, he had light brown hair, a medium frame and a diffident, slightly lopsided smile. He wore well-cut gray slacks and a light tweed jacket over a blue oxford shirt unbuttoned at the neck.

"Sorry just to walk in, but the door was open and I *did* knock." He pantomimed knocking with the knobbed cane he carried. "Good evening, Mr. Honeycutt; welcome back to Colleton County, Kate."

Lacy gave a formal nod, but Kate crossed the parlor with outstretched hands and impulsively clasped his.

"Gordon!" she said, conscious of his double loss since they'd last met. "How good to see you again. I almost didn't recognize you without your beard."

"The nurses shaved it off after the accident," said Gordon Tyrrell, "and it wouldn't grow back properly, so I've had to get acquainted with a razor again."

He bent to kiss her cheek in greeting and she saw the long smooth scar. It followed his strong left jawline and was almost unnoticeable now, but it would undoubtedly stand out in white relief if he tried to grow a beard around it.

"You look very nice without it," Kate smiled.

And he did. Younger, too, and somehow more vulnerable. In the few times they'd been thrown together over the past four or five years, Gordon had always struck her as very Old South—ever aware that the blood of a heroic Confederate colonel flowed in his veins, but ready to be polite to the granddaughter of Irish immigrants since she was the wife of his own wife's cousin. Without Elaine's vivacity to play against now, and bereft of his precisely clipped beard, he seemed more human and less standoffish.

"Can I help with that?" he asked, eyeing the sideboard.

"Oh, no," said Kate. "You shouldn't—"

"Because of the cane?" Gordon asked. "That's mainly for show. My leg's almost completely healed."

He laid the stick aside and with all three of them shoving, the sideboard edged another six inches closer to the door.

"This isn't working," said Kate, "and we're wrecking the floor. The movers are bound to have a dolly or something and I'll get them to shift it tomorrow. Come and sit down, Gordon. Can I get you a drink?"

"Actually, I came to offer you one," he said. "Dinner, too. Much against her will, Mrs. Faircloth's cooked a whole leg of lamb, and there's just Mary Pat and me. We'd be very honored if you and Mr. Honeycutt would join us."

"Thank you kindly," said Lacy, who'd never tasted lamb till Kate came, "but I reckon I'd better hang around here. Dogs ain't been fed yet and there's still some chores need doing." His voice trailed off.

The thought of spending the whole evening with Lacy's taciturnity was suddenly more than Kate wanted to face.

"I'd love to come," she said. "What time?"

"Now," said Gordon. "Mary Pat's still a little young for more formal hours. I'll wait if you want to change."

"I won't be more than ten minutes," Kate promised. "Lacy, there's a chicken casserole on the stove, if you want it."

Without waiting to hear his rebuff, Kate hurried down the hall to her room and kicked off her sneakers. She had not forgotten the quick-change tricks she had learned as a model and in precisely nine and a half minutes, she had showered, brushed her hair into an elegant twist, and slipped into low heels and a short cream-colored skirt topped by an oversized pullover of pale blue, green, and lavender cotton that brought out the blue of her changeable eyes and disguised her thickened waistline.

"Beautiful," said Gordon as she came back along the hall with a white shawl draped over her shoulder in case the night turned chilly. "Elaine never made a huge mystical production about changing either. She could go from a boat deck to a ballroom in less time than it took most women to decide what shade of lipstick to wear."

As Gordon held the door for her, Kate paused and said, "Gordon, forgive me, but I must tell you how sorry I am about Elaine and James. Jake and I both were."

He closed the door and looked down into her earnest face. "It was a hellish autumn for both of us, wasn't it, Kate?"

His lopsided grin was wobbly but he took a deep breath as he straightened and walked around the car to slide in beside her. He put the key in the ignition but did not immediately turn it.

"When Rob Bryant called to tell me about Jake, I couldn't believe it. I'd just had a letter from him three days before. Kate, you must know that if I hadn't still been laid up in that Mexican hospital—"

"I know," she said quickly. "The flowers you sent were so beautiful. Did you—I mean, what about Elaine and James?"

"In late October—after the doctors finally let me out of the hospital—there was a little church near our villa that Elaine used to stop in at once in a while. I'm afraid none of us were very religious, but I think she and James would have liked the memorial service.

"There were services for the others, too. Seven other people, Kate. The Dickersons, Jill and Win Harkness, friends the three of us had known for years. Gone. And then to hear that Jake—"

He switched on the ignition, put the Porsche in gear, and eased into the lane. "All I could think about was how James had saved his life in Vietnam, and then a freakish accident on his own land, with his own gun!"

"I know," Kate said bleakly.

"And now this," said Gordon as they drove slowly past the packhouse.

"Did James talk about Vietnam much?" Kate asked.

"Occasionally. Especially when he first came home. Not so much in recent years."

"Do you remember the other two who were on that patrol? A younger man and a Bernie-somebody?"

"Yes, he mentioned them. Why?"

"The man Mary Pat and I found—you didn't see him, did you?"

"No, but Detective Bryant described him; asked if anyone at Gilead had seen him around. He didn't sound like anyone . . . wait a minute! Bernie? Was *he* the man who was killed?"

"It could be," said Kate. "I never met him, but Jake told me about that patrol and how Bernie and James killed the sniper. And there were pictures. He had a black mole on his right cheek, too, just like the dead man, only he had a beard back then. Lacy's misplaced the snapshots Jake sent him, but I think there may be duplicates in the things the movers are bringing tomorrow."

"It's probably not him," said Gordon. "Why would he turn up here after all these years?"

"Maybe he came to see Jake. Not knowing."

They paused at the top of the lane to wait for a huge, late-working tractor to pass. The sky blazed with silver pricks of stars everywhere except where blanked out by Raleigh's glow in the north. The new moon was a pristine crescent against the blue-black of the western sky. They crossed the highway. Gilead's long drive was lined on either side by double rows of tall oaks which were just beginning to push out tiny leaves.

"Odd business," Gordon said thoughtfully. "Did you tell Bryant?"

"Yes, he's coming back tomorrow to see if I can find the pictures."

Gordon drove past the white pillars of the wide veranda and on around to the study entrance on the west side.

"You know," he said, cutting off the switch, "there's a trunk of James's things in the attic. I remember he had a little chest of war souvenirs. It might give us more information about Bernie. I'll have a look tomorrow."

The study had a low wide window and they saw Mary Pat slip into the room and look out at them shyly.

"There's the reason I've had to put death behind me and pick up the pieces," said Gordon. "Children do make a difference, Kate."

"I'm counting on it." The huskiness of her voice made him look at her quizzically. "Yes," she nodded.

His lopsided grin widened into a delighted smile. "That's wonderful!" he exclaimed and his smile grew as he circled the car to help her out. "Truly wonderful."

"What is?" asked Mary Pat from the doorway.

Chapter
Seven

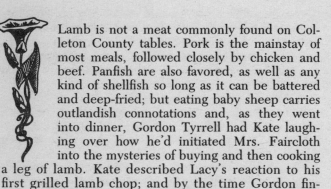Lamb is not a meat commonly found on Colleton County tables. Pork is the mainstay of most meals, followed closely by chicken and beef. Panfish are also favored, as well as any kind of shellfish so long as it can be battered and deep-fried; but eating baby sheep carries outlandish connotations and, as they went into dinner, Gordon Tyrrell had Kate laughing over how he'd initiated Mrs. Faircloth into the mysteries of buying and then cooking a leg of lamb. Kate described Lacy's reaction to his first grilled lamb chop; and by the time Gordon finished carving, Mary Pat had lost her shyness of Kate and was peppering the dinner with questions about the baby.

"But *when* will it come?" she asked again, her brown eyes sparkling with excitement.

"In four more months—around the Fourth of July," said Kate. "Independence Day will probably be my last day of independence."

Mary Pat looked puzzled and there was a brief digression as Gordon tried to explain the significance of the Fourth and American independence.

He was extraordinarily patient with the child, thought Kate approvingly. Although Mary Pat displayed the precocity of most children raised in the company of adults, she seemed unspoiled. The conversation was geared to her level and her questions were taken seriously, but she was not allowed to monopolize.

Seated beneath the crystal chandelier, the little girl looked more like Park Avenue tonight than Tobacco Road. Her dark curls were brushed to a sheen, parted on the side, and held back from her face with a delicate cloisonné barrette. Instead of scuffed sneakers, she wore black patent-leather Mary Janes and long white socks, and her scruffy knit slacks and pullover had been replaced by a white batiste dress smocked with green threads and laced at the waist with a thin green velvet ribbon.

Her small face was a blend of her parents' best features, and when she cut her eyes at Kate without moving her head as Patricia once had, or when her lips quirked in one of Philip's smiles, Kate was captivated.

"You know one nice thing about my baby?" she told Mary Pat. "You two will be double cousins."

"What's that?" the child asked.

"It means you share great-grandfathers on both sides."

Mary Pat was startled. "Sides?" she asked, looking down at both elbows.

"Let's see you explain that," said Gordon, amused.

Kate requested paper and pen and the maid produced them.

"Southerners aren't the only ones who keep their bloodlines straight," Kate said, and hoped she would remember all that Miss Emily had told her that morning.

Mary Pat slipped from her chair and came to stand by Kate's shoulder.

"Let's say this is you," said Kate, sketching in a

small stick figure with twin ponytails. "And this is the baby."

On the other side of the sheet appeared a bundle with a tiny smiling face.

"Here are your mother and father, and here're Jake and me."

"Will you die, too, after the baby comes?"

"No, sweetheart," she said before Gordon could admonish Mary Pat.

"Now here's your grandfather Franklin Gilbert and your great-grandfather Gilbert. Where you have grandfather Franklin, the baby has grandmother Jane. Jane and Franklin were brother and sister and had the same daddy. Your mother and Jake were first cousins so you and the baby will be second cousins on your Gilbert side. Got that?" she asked as her pencil deftly sketched amusing little stick figures.

Mary Pat nodded.

"Okay. Your dad and my mother had the same grandfather Carmichael, so you and I are second cousins and the baby will be your second cousin once-removed on the Carmichael side!" Kate finished triumphantly.

"Bravo!" Gordon applauded and lifted his wine glass in toast.

Mary Pat carried the tablet to the other end of the table. "Where are you, Uncle Gordon?"

Gordon touched the Patricia figure with the pencil tip. "This is your mother, right?"

"Yes, sir."

"I can't draw as well as Cousin Kate, but we'll let this be Aunt Elaine next to your mother because they were sisters. Then we draw double lines from Aunt Elaine to me and put me in here like this because we were married."

"Do Uncle James, too, please."

Patiently, Gordon drew in the figure and lines that included his brother on the crowded chart.

Kate began to regret that she'd brought up the subject of kinship, but if Gordon was pained by this mention of James and Elaine, he hid it from his niece.

"No, honey, we can't put lines to Sally. She's not kin. But here's Uncle Lacy."

The entrance of dessert sent Mary Pat back to her chair. Their conversation turned to kittens and Kate invited her to come back the next afternoon to find the kitten Lacy had given her.

"We'll have coffee in the study," Gordon told the maid and as they left the dining room, Sally Whitley appeared on the landing above.

She gave Kate a shy smile and beckoned to Mary Pat. "Time to get ready for bed."

"Off you go," said Gordon.

Still carrying the tablet, Mary Pat scampered up the wide carpeted stairs. "Guess what, Sally? I'm going to have a second cousin on both sides!"

"I hope you're prepared for the whole neighborhood to know," Gordon laughed as they entered the study.

It was a welcoming room. Books lined the fireplace wall and a fire in the hearth banished the slight chill that had appeared after the sun went down. The lamps cast mellow pools of light upon a faded oriental rug and over comfortable leather chairs and couches.

The maid—Kate thought she was one of Bessie Stewart's nieces, but she wasn't sure—followed with the coffee tray and then withdrew.

Gordon brought a bottle from a side cabinet. "Brandy in yours?"

"No, thank you. I probably shouldn't even be drinking this much coffee. I will join you in a cigarette, though."

He held a light for both of them. "I should think cigarettes would be verboten."

"They are," she sighed. "I've cut down to less than half a pack a day, but I just can't seem to quit altogether. Especially after a meal when there's someone to talk to. And *that*," she added grimly, "is the first positive thing about life with Lacy Honeycutt that I've come up with. After a week of facing him at every meal, I'll probably be cured of ever wanting another cigarette."

"Don't be bitter, Kate. It's been rough on him, too."

She shrugged and Gordon stooped to put another log on the fire. He seemed awkward for a moment.

"Was it the left leg you broke?" she asked.

Gordon nodded. "It's pretty much healed, but the doctors said I could expect some continuing weakness there for at least a year. I've acquired quite a collection of canes for my old age. Midge and Knowland Whaley— did you ever meet them?"

Kate shook her head.

"They sent me a gold-headed cane from Cannes and Sean Riley—"

"A redheaded Irishman with a professional brogue?"

"The same. He turned up at the hospital in Mexico with an authentic shillelagh. I was still pretty groggy, bandaged from head to foot like King Tut's mummy, but damned if he didn't make me laugh before the nurses chased him out."

"How long were you actually in the hospital?"

"Eight weeks total, I think it was. From early September to late October. The concussion kept me in a coma for almost ten days."

He fingered the scar along his jawline. "This took twelve stitches, they tell me."

Kate made a sympathetic sound.

"The worst thing about it is that the whole day was wiped out of my memory."

Gordon resumed his seat on the couch and stared into the flames. "I remember dinner on the terrace the evening before. James and the Harknesses were spending a few days with us and Cyrus Dickerson called and invited us to go sailing the next day. It was a ninety-footer, teak deck—beautiful thing. Crew of three. The Harknesses loved messing about in boats. Jill's father was one of the stewards at Newport.

"And I can remember someone saying 'red skies in the morning' because the sun came up a bit pink, but after that, it's all a blank. Concussion does that, I'm told. Erases the most recent memories.

"There was a McDermott woman, Cyrus's friend, who filled me in on the actual squall—the lines tangled and the mast snapped before they could reef the mainsail. It was total confusion, she said, and she doesn't recall the exact sequence of events or even who was where. One of the crew members survived, too, but his memory's just as spotty."

"Is it important?" Kate asked gently.

"Yes, it is rather. You see, Kate," he said apologetically, "I don't know if I was a hero or a coward. How did I manage to save myself and not save Elaine or my brother?"

"No Tyrrell could ever be a coward," said Kate and it was, miraculously, the right thing to say.

Gordon gave her a grateful smile and they began to speak of Kate's plans to remodel the packhouse.

"Unless you have someone specific in mind, you're welcome to use Tom Whitley," he offered.

"Doesn't Gilead keep him busy?"

"When summer comes, it probably will. Just mowing the lawns takes two full days as I recall, but most of the farm's leased and there's little grounds work right now. He's supposed to be quite handy with a hammer and saw, and I gather they could use the extra money."

"Are the Whitleys local?"

"No, California, I think. Ever since Patricia died, Gilead's caretakers have been State University kids, so I assume Whitley was recommended through the school's financial aid office and Rob Bryant vetted him for the trustees. In fact, Rob staffed the whole place when I told him Mary Pat and I were coming back to Gilead. Then at the last minute, the Mexican nursemaid balked at coming north, so Sally stepped into the breach. It was supposed to be temporary, but Mary Pat's taken to her, and the doctor says we shouldn't introduce any more change than is absolutely necessary."

"Miss Emily mentioned Mary Pat's trouble," Kate said.

"She's getting better. Fewer nightmares. But she still believes things can change their appearances overnight."

"Like the kitten," said Kate.

"Kitten?"

"That's how she came to be with me when I found the body. Lacy gave her a kitten and she brought it back because she said her kitten had white feet and that one's feet were different. They all look the same to me."

"They probably are," Gordon sighed. "At Christmas, I—or rather Santa Claus—gave her some bedroom slippers shaped like little rabbits. She loved them. Wore them all day long for three days, then got up on the fourth morning and declared they weren't the same bunnies. Their spots were different, she said, and since then she won't touch them."

Through the open doorway, they saw a flash of white on the staircase and Mary Pat in pajamas and fuzzy pink slippers darted across the hall. She paused upon the threshold, suddenly shy again.

Gordon held out his hand. "Did you come to say goodnight to Cousin Kate?"

"Yes, sir," she answered in the way of well-mannered Southern children. The corners of her mouth tilted upward. "And will you tell me a story?" she asked winningly.

"Not tonight," he began, but Kate forestalled him.

"You mustn't change bedtime ritual on my account. It's been a long day and bed begins to sound like a wonderful idea to me, too."

She stood and Gordon patted his pants pocket. Car keys jingled. "Let me run you home then," he said as they walked out into the entrance hall.

"Nonsense. It's a warm night and I need to walk off some of that delicious dinner. Tomorrow's my first appointment with an obstetrician in Raleigh and she'll probably lecture me about exercise and weight."

"You aren't nervous about walking through the lane alone?" Gordon asked as the maid appeared with Kate's shawl.

"Because of the—" She started to say murder but stopped as she realized that Mary Pat was listening to their words.

"Well," said Gordon. "After all . . ."

"I doubt if he's lurking around," she said dryly.

The maid held her shawl. Kate thanked her and slung it loosely about her shoulders before stooping to Mary Pat's level. "Goodnight, sweetheart."

The child gave her a quick spontaneous hug, then retreated to Gordon's legs. He swung her up on his back in an easy movement and hooked his arms under her legs to hold her in place while Mary Pat clasped her arms around his neck.

As they lingered a moment on the wide veranda, Mary Pat rested her head on Gordon's shoulder and sang softly and dreamily to herself, a song about a spotted pony galloping, galloping.

"At least give me a call when you get home," said Gordon. "If you don't phone in a half hour, I'll come looking for you."

She laughed and set off briskly down the drive. The night air was a little too cool for ambling, but she knew it would be comfortable once her blood stirred.

Even though the moon was less than first quarter, it gave sufficient light after her eyes were accustomed to the darkness. The gravel drive was quite visible now since the oaks above them had no leaves to block even a pale moon. Azaleas kept their leaves all year through, however, and were bulky dark masses beyond the oaks, impenetrable in their inkiness. Whole armies could camp there, thought Kate, without her seeing them.

Yet she wasn't consciously nervous. The dead man had a likeness to Jake's old army buddy; but until he was definitely identified as such, she could consider him a stranger, killed in her isolated packhouse for reasons that were nothing to do with her. Surely the killer had no cause to return.

She came to the highway, crossed, and entered the sandy lane. The westering moon dodged in and out of the pine tops as she passed silently along the rutted track.

Night sounds in the country were quieter, but no less varied than in a city. Wind, pushed through longleaf pines, made soughing murmurs as steady as any flow of traffic. Spring peepers were loud in the creek bottom; dogs barked in the distance; and an occasional car passed on the highway, a burst of music from its radio trailing behind.

To the southeast, a line of Marine Corps helicopters, practicing night maneuvers, flop-flopped slowly across the sky like a string of lost Christmas tree lights looking for a giant tannenbaum. When the sound of their rotors had faded, Kate heard the end of a plaintive bird cry in the wooded triangle to her right. Owl? She knew it was still too early for a chuck-will's-widow.

She listened intently, but the cry was not repeated.

At the bottom of the slope, the packhouse loomed up darkly beside the lane, its one window like a black eyepatch on the north side peering out at her.

Kate had just drawn even with it when her blood froze at the sudden awareness of another presence. Footsteps approached stealthily from behind the packhouse.

She heard dead leaves crunch beneath someone's feet, a slight scuffling of twigs brushed against the wall, and she became rigid, unable to breathe.

"Lacy?" she whispered.

Silence.

"Who's there?" she said tremulously.

The scuffling became louder and closer.

She drew back to run just as the dogs burst through the bushes and tumbled into the lane to greet her. Shaky with relief, Kate realized that they had caught her scent and come down from the yard to meet her.

She bent to scratch behind their ears and let them nuzzle her face and a cold shock of reality flowed through her. Part of her desire to walk home alone was to prove to herself that the morning's shakes had been a passing condition.

The dogs had just shown her that her nerves were not as steady as she'd thought.

She was still feeling edgy as the dogs escorted her through the orchard, although the area light mounted

on a pole near the kitchen porch made another surprise
like the dogs unlikely.

Up in the yard, an unfamiliar dark green truck was
parked under the light. It had a larger cab than the
usual pickup and its longer bed had no side panels,
only a row of what looked to Kate like four or five
fenceposts on either edge of the flatbed. There was
some sort of homemade winch immediately behind the
cab and double rear wheels supported the flatbed.

A low murmur of masculine voices reached her ears
and when Kate passed the truck to approach the back
porch, she saw Lacy and another man leaning against
the truck in deep conversation.

The other man spotted Kate first when she was
about forty feet away. "Evening, ma'am," he said.

Lacy straightened abruptly.

Kate gave the formal nod she knew was expected
and would have continued on into the house had not
Lacy suddenly become mannerly for the first time since
she'd arrived.

"This here's Tucker Sauls," he said. "He's gonna
help me haul out some of them firewood logs."

Tucker Sauls was cut from the same mold as Lacy:
tall and bony and just as wrinkled, but with the same
impression of wiry strength. He lifted his crumpled old
fedora and the light overhead revealed a bald head.
"Evening, ma'am," he repeated.

Kate was momentarily confused, not wanting to vio-
late the delicate mores of country courtesies. Did Lacy
expect her to join them by the truck?

She slowed her steps and acknowledged the intro-
duction with a friendly smile and pleasantries about the
spring night even as she kept moving toward the back
porch.

Evidently, it was the correct response, for she saw
Lacy relax against the truck side as she said goodnight
and entered the house.

She went to the telephone and called Gilead, and,

when a maid answered, asked that Gordon be told she'd returned safely.

By then Kate was so tired that she went straight to bed and was already drifting off to sleep when she heard the old truck outside crank up and lumber on down the lane.

Chapter Eight

The Alberta Clipper roared out of Canada that night to glaze the Midwest with yet another layer of ice and snow and to dump ten inches on winter-weary New York. By the time it reached central Carolina some time after midnight, though, its power was diffused. The mercury dipped into the upper twenties as winds shifted from southeast to northwest, but the sun came up on clear skies and forecasters were predicting temperatures in the low fifties.

"A beautiful March day for Greensboro," burbled the announcer.

"How nice for Greensboro," thought Kate and switched off the bedside radio with only a fleeting wonder as to why a Raleigh station would report on weather ninety miles to the west.

She had awakened with boundless energy and by nine o'clock, her first load of laundry was flapping in the breeze and the old automatic washer in the kitchen was chugging through a second load of overalls and flannel shirts that she'd practically wrestled away from Lacy.

"I can do my own washing," he told her.

"I know you can, Lacy, but I have some jeans and things that won't make a full load, so why waste the hot water?" she asked, determined that Lacy would not spoil her good mood.

His thrift appealed to, Lacy had grudgingly complied.

"I've started a grocery list on the counter," she told him. "If you want to add anything, I have an appointment in Raleigh and I'll shop afterwards."

The telephone rang and she hurried down the hall, thinking they really could use a couple of extensions.

"Good morning, Cousin Katie," came Rob Bryant's cheerful voice over the wire. "Mother tells me you'll be in town this afternoon. Why don't you come a little early and let me take you to lunch?"

"I haven't spoken to your mother since lunch yesterday," Kate laughed, "so how did she know?"

"I never question Mother's sources. Nor her facts. She isn't wrong this time, is she? You will come in for lunch, won't you?"

"I'd love to, Rob, but the movers haven't arrived, so I couldn't give you a definite time."

"That's okay," he said. "We didn't schedule much for today. Come when you can. I'll wait for you."

By mid-morning, the brisk sunny day had dried the laundry, and as Kate folded sheets and shirts out by the clothesline, the dogs gave friendly woofs of warning and she turned to see a blue Toyota pickup drive into the yard with Mary Pat holding on tightly in the back.

Gordon emerged from the passenger seat as if from a Rolls. Despite plaid flannel shirt, corduroy slacks and brown wool sweater, he couldn't help looking faintly patrician as he presented the Toyota's driver to Kate, who left her laundry basket on the kitchen porch and came forward to meet them.

Tom Whitley was older than she'd expected. Instead of a college kid, he was perhaps in his mid-twenties, a sharp-featured young man with a shock of dark brown hair and deep-set brown eyes that met and then darted away from Kate's. He wore jeans and a denim windbreaker and had the nervous intensity of a man more at ease with things than people. "Mr. Tyrrell says you need some work done."

"And he tells me you're a good carpenter," Kate smiled, instinctively trying to put him at ease.

"I'm a pretty fair jackleg," he said, looking over her head. It was impossible for Kate to hold his eyes. He spoke to the air just left of her face or to the sleeve of her sweater. He kept one hand in his pocket and Kate heard the nervous tinkling of loose change against his key ring.

"Perhaps you'd like to see the place," Kate suggested kindly.

The four of them walked through the orchard to the packhouse accompanied by the two pointers and Aunt Susie, a mostly beagle bitch who patiently withstood Mary Pat's hugs and ear-scratches.

While Kate outlined her plans for a studio, Whitley took a screwdriver from his back pocket and poked and pried at the rotten wood beneath the north window. He lifted the trapdoor, pushed the curious dogs aside so that he could examine the joists from below, and pronounced the floor basically sound. Kate described the counters she wanted built and Whitley looked at the top button on her shirt and made some suggestions about rewiring and plumbing.

"If you're not in too big a hurry, I can work this in around my school schedule and on weekends, and probably be finished in two weeks if that's all right with you and Mr. Tyrrell."

"Take all the time you need," Gordon said.

"Gordon, are you sure?" asked Kate. "I don't want to impose."

"You're not imposing. Tom's conscientious about Gilead, but there just isn't enough to keep him busy until summer, is there, Tom?"

Before he could answer, Mary Pat appeared at the

open door with a kitten cradled in each arm and said, "Cousin Kate, Uncle Lacy's calling you. Your truck's come."

"I *will* impose now," said Kate and described the heavy chest that needed to be shifted.

The movers soon had Kate's cartons, drawing table, and few pieces of furniture stowed in the front parlor; then they hoisted the sideboard up on their dolly and, with Tom Whitley's help, muscled it to one of the unused bedrooms upstairs. Kate had just signed the final voucher and sent the movers on their way with a generous tip when the phone rang.

"Dwight Bryant," Lacy called down the hall.

"Oh, dear! He's going to ask about that man's name," said Kate. "Gordon, do you mind? Look for the carton marked with Jake's name, okay?"

She darted along to the telephone and heard Dwight drawl, "Morning, Kate. Wonder if you've had a chance to find those pictures of Jake's yet?"

"The cartons just came. Hang on a few minutes."

She hurried back to the front parlor.

"Is this the one?" asked Gordon, pushing aside some of the boxes so Kate could get closer.

"That's it." She began to tear at the tape that held the cardboard box together.

"Here, let me," said Tom Whitley. He took out a pocket knife and sliced through the tape.

The top fell open and Kate rummaged among books and papers. "You didn't look through James's trunk yet, did you, Gordon?"

"No, it completely slipped my mind. I'll go up to the attic this afternoon."

The bulky manila envelope she sought was halfway down and, since Dwight was waiting on the telephone, Kate just upended it into the carton.

Letters, draft papers, military forms, a battle ribbon, part of a torn army terrain map, and some odds and ends with Vietnamese printing tumbled out. Mixed in were a handful of snapshots and negatives. Kate hastily riffled through them until she found the one she had remembered, a picture of Jake with three companions. On the reverse was his round scrawl: "Nam '70 w/Tyrrell, Covington & W.T."

Like James, Jake had occasionally worn a mustache in Vietnam, only he had shaved his off permanently when their tour of duty was over. Kate had to look carefully to distinguish her husband's face from his friend's. The difference in height helped. Bernie Covington's beard was as full as she remembered; the youngest man's face was indistinct.

"Sorry to keep you waiting," Kate apologized to Dwight Bryant a moment later. The dim hall blurred the snapshot's details. "It really doesn't look much like the man in the packhouse. The mole's the same, but I can't tell a thing about his features because of the beard. Anyhow, I was close—the name is Covington, not Chesterton."

She spelled it for him. "I have to go out this afternoon, but if you want the picture, I can leave it with Lacy."

"Well, the name's the important thing," said Dwight. "With his fingerprints and a name, we can go ahead and see what the army knows about him. If it's all the same to you, I'll pick up the picture tomorrow morning sometime."

"Okay," Kate agreed.

She returned to the parlor and put the snapshots back in the envelope with Jake's other service souvenirs.

"Dwight Bryant says he'll come for it tomorrow," she said.

"Bet he don't budge ten feet from a television the rest of the day," Lacy said with what was almost a chuckle.

Gordon glanced at his watch and announced that it was high time he and Mary Pat went home for lunch.

Kate thanked them for their help and Tom Whitley almost met her eyes as he promised to return the next day, Saturday, and help figure out what materials they should order from the lumber company.

When they had gone, Kate finished taking in the laundry; and as she passed through the kitchen, she found Lacy heating a can of soup for his lunch, the television turned to some sporting event. She showered and put on a favorite plaid silk dress in tones of jade. It should have bloused more at the waist, but with a navy linen blazer, she didn't look too pregnant. Even so, it might be time to check out some maternity clothes, she decided.

When she stepped back in the kitchen to pick up the grocery list, Lacy barely acknowledged her departure over the roar of the frenzied television crowd.

The drive to Raleigh took about thirty-five minutes and was a pleasant meander along back roads past dandelions, purple henbit, patches of blue Quaker-ladies, and white Johnny-jump-ups. In June and July, the ditchbanks would be thick with orange daylilies and clumps of butterfly weed; blue cornflowers would run through fields of grain; then autumn would bring blue asters and purple shooting stars beneath early-turning trees. Kate loved how wildflowers marked the seasons along this country road that turned and twisted and eventually brought her through a large dairy farm at the southwest edge of town, a dairy farm owned by North Carolina State University.

The university's curriculum was heavily weighted with science, technology, and computer engineering; but it had begun as an agricultural school and, even though it was no longer a cow college as Duke and Chapel Hill students teased, it would never shake off its origins—witness the several hundred black and white cows that still grazed on rolling green meadows and ignored the passing cars.

Despite its growth, Raleigh remained an easy town to drive through. Street parking was a problem in midtown since Fayetteville Street had been converted to a pedestrian mall; but in the Cameron Village section where Rob Bryant practiced law, Kate found several empty spaces outside his office building.

Against all professional procedures with which Kate was familiar, the firm's receptionist had a tiny portable television on her desk. She turned down the audio as Kate approached, but her eyes flickered toward the picture.

"Mr. Bryant, please," Kate said.

"He's in conference right now," she smiled. "Is he expecting you?"

"Yes, he is. I'm Mrs. Honeycutt."

The young woman glanced again at the television. "Carolina's ahead of Clemson by five," she grinned, "and here's the commercial. I'll see if Mr. Bryant's free."

She rose and disappeared around the corner. In a couple of moments she reappeared, followed by Rob.

"Kate! Come on back and let me introduce you to everybody. You met Debby, didn't you? Debby Mizner, Kate Honeycutt."

They exchanged polite smiles.

"Rob, I don't want to interrupt you if—"

"No interruption," he said, hurrying her down the hall. "It's two minutes till the half, though."

He opened the door to a formal conference room. The chairs along the glass-topped table were occupied by eight or ten people with soft drinks, coffee cups, and various take-out lunches; smells of pizza sauce, fried chicken, and deli pastrami mingled in the air. At the end of the room was a large color television, and Kate saw a basketball court awash with pale blue and white uniforms and excited cheerleaders waving blue pompoms.

"Okay, you people. Drag your eyes off the screen a minute. This is Cousin Kate from New York," Rob said.

A friendly chorus greeted Kate, but Rob's exhortation to his colleagues was useless.

"Can you believe Matt Doherty today?" exclaimed

a young woman who was otherwise a dress-for-success
model of a tailored-down, buttoned-up attorney.

"Yeah," chimed one of her male counterparts who
was dabbing at a mustard stain on his tie. "You expect
Sam Perkins or Michael Jordan to make those super
shots, but Doherty?"

"It was the Duke game that did it," said one of the
gray-haired senior partners magisterially.

"He's had the potential all year," agreed another
partner who had also graduated from Carolina.

"A flash in the pan," the one Duke alumnus in the
room said gamely. "Duke took 'em to two overtimes
last Saturday and I bet we edge by tomorrow."

Jeers went up at his heresy and as the buzzer sounded
for the end of the first half, everything suddenly fell into
place for Kate: it was basketball tournament time for the
Atlantic Coast Conference—a spring madness almost in-
comprehensible to newcomers or outsiders.

With Duke, Wake Forest, Carolina, and North Carolina State within spitting distance of each other, and
with no professional teams to engage their enthusiasm,
North Carolinians picked a college team to which they
remained loyal from birth to death. It was exactly like
being born into a political party or a religion, Kate had
decided. If your family were State fans, you grew up
one, too. You wore a little red T-shirt with a wolf on
the front when you were a baby, you bristled at the
sight of other babies in Carolina blue T-shirts, and both
of you learned early to yell, "Nuke DOOK!" when
egged on by the adults in your respective families.

When you grew up, your car would sport bumper
stickers that read "Phi Packa Attacka" or "If God's not
a Tar Heel, why's the sky Carolina blue?"

And once a year, when ACC Tournament weekend
rolled around, if you were not a heavily-contributing
alumnus—the twenty thousand or so tickets were split
among the eight colleges and were never, *ever* sold
to the general public—you settled in with a group of
similarly-aligned friends for three days of intensive television viewing.

This year's tournament was at the Greensboro Coliseum, which was why, Kate realized, the radio announcer this morning had been so happy about Greensboro's weather. This was also why Lacy had turned on the television for lunch, why Rob's firm had kept the afternoon clear, and why Dwight Bryant might not be seen till Monday morning.

As she recalled from earlier years, there were four games the first day, two the second, and the championship game on Sunday. For three days, every business office, department store, restaurant, you name it, would suddenly sprout portable televisions and radios.

"Don't employers *mind?*" Kate asked as she and Rob drove to a nearby restaurant.

"Most employers are in Greensboro this weekend," he said. "And those that aren't are hanging over a television, too."

The restaurant was uncrowded and they were seated right away.

"So," Kate said, resigned to the inevitable sports talk, "is Carolina going to win?"

"I guaran-damn-tee you, as Lacy would say. They're unbeaten in conference play. Of course, Duke gave them a scare last Saturday and Maryland's hungry to win a championship for Lefty Driesell, but Carolina has two All-Americans."

Rob brushed at a cowlick of russet hair and laughed at the polite tilt of her head. He had heard the resignation in her voice.

"Poor Kate! You really did pick a bad time to come, didn't you? Dead bodies in your packhouse, wall-to-wall basketball for the next three days. Depending on how many ACC teams get picked for the NCAA, you may not get anybody to talk about politics, the Middle East, or even prayer in the public schools till after the first of April!"

"Murder takes second place, too," she said, and told Rob of his brother's decision to wait till the next day to pick up the picture of Bernie Covington.

"You have to remember that Dwight helped win a

basketball championship in our high school division. Once a player, always a fan."

"You didn't play?"

"Oh, I played. My team just didn't have the same talent as Dwight's. We finished third every time."

"Was it hard having a brother you couldn't match?" Kate asked shrewdly.

"Do I sound jealous?" His slanted green eyes were rueful. "You know, Dwight could have played for Carolina. The recruiters were interested, but he wanted to join the army, see the world. When I got over to Chapel Hill, I couldn't even make junior varsity." He grinned at her and the playful fox look returned to his pointed face. "Sibling rivalry's a dreadful thing, Kate. Be grateful you're an only child. You ready to order?"

Kate prudently chose a salad plate and glass of white wine. Rob opted for a steak sandwich and beer.

"Who's Bernie Covington, anyhow?" he asked. "And why does Dwight want his picture?"

Kate had forgotten that Rob hadn't been there when Lacy remembered that Jake's old army acquaintance also had a prominent black mole on his right cheek. "Miss Emily must be slipping," she teased when she had explained.

"Dwight must have gone straight back to Dobbs," Rob agreed. "On the other hand, he's one of the few people who can spend an hour with Mother and leave knowing more than he's told."

"Like what's happened to his marriage?" Kate guessed.

Rob nodded. "He's hurting, but all he'll say is that Jonna likes Washington better than she likes Dobbs and that the divorce will be final this summer if they can agree on custody and visitation for young Cal. I offered to handle it for him, but he told me to butt out and I did."

His tone was light, but Kate sensed the hurt.

"Anyhow," she said, steering the conversation back to less personal ground, "Lacy mislaid the snapshots

Jake sent him years ago, but I found copies in the things that came today."

"Was it the same man?"

Kate shrugged. "It would be quite a coincidence, wouldn't it?"

Their food arrived and as they ate, Kate mused, "Odd how much difference a beard makes. I can't get used to Gordon without his, can you?"

"I hardly knew him," said Rob. "You heard Mother: once Gordon and Elaine married, they took off for more exotic climes. Colleton County was too provincial for them. I doubt if I ever saw him or his brother, either, more than two or three times in the last few years and that was always at a party or some sort of mob scene where you can't speak to anyone except at a shout. I've only come to know Gordon since Thanksgiving. I do know I've heard Mother and Bessie talk that when Jake tried to play matchmaker, it was between James and Elaine, not Gordon. Jake ever mention it?"

"I'd forgotten all about that," said Kate, "but you're right. It was after Vietnam. They were all back in college then and James came down for spring break. Jake told me he thought James and Elaine might click, but nothing ever happened. Then Gordon tagged along the summer Patricia and Philip were married and it was love at first sight."

According to Bessie Stewart, the first sight of a millionaire brother-in-law probably hadn't hurt either. True or not, thought Rob, Elaine and Gordon had seemed perfectly matched: both had proper bloodlines and Elaine's allowance from Patricia was large enough to finance the sort of life they wanted. Even Bessie and his mother approved of how devoted to each other Elaine and Gordon appeared.

He wondered aloud why James had never married.

"Jake said he couldn't afford to," said Kate. "There was a small trust fund somewhere. Enough to keep him off the unemployment line, but not enough to support a wife in the style-to-which, et cetera. I think that's why they had drifted apart by the time Jake met me.

You know what a workaholic Jake could be. He just couldn't understand a man not settling down to a real career, and James seemed to be the perpetual houseguest. Always the extra man to balance Elaine's table.

"They kept in touch, though—met for drinks when James was passing through town, and he came over for dinner once right after we were married; but I think Jake was disappointed in the way James's life was turning out, even though he never said so."

Jake's loyalty to people and places was another of the things Kate missed with aching sorrow.

To change the subject and take away the sad look in her eyes, Rob said, "I hear you're ready to start remodeling the packhouse tomorrow?"

Her lips widened in a slow smile. "Is that maid at Gilead by any chance one of Bessie Stewart's nieces?"

"DeWanda Lanelle Sanders," he admitted with one of his small tight grins. "She's got a sister if you need someone to help out this spring."

"Gordon told me that you'd staffed Gilead. I'm surprised you hired outsiders like the Whitleys."

Rob finished his sandwich and shook his head when the waiter suggested another beer. "It's hard to get someone local who'll live in," he said, "and the trustees don't like to leave Gilead without someone on the premises. The college has been good about finding responsible prospects, although—come to think of it—it was Whitley who approached me last fall. He was recommended by the grad student who'd had it before him."

"Is Tom Whitley a graduate student, too?" she asked, sipping the last of her wine.

"Because he's older? No. He dropped out of high school and ran away to the army. I believe he got an equivalency diploma in the service, and last spring decided not to make a military career, but come east and study horticulture or landscaping instead. His wife's a kindergarten teacher, you know, so it worked out perfectly when Gordon needed an emergency nursemaid for Mary Pat. You're sure you don't want another glass of wine?"

"And go reeling into my obstetrician's office? No, thank you." She glanced at her watch and saw that it was nearly time for her appointment.

Rob called for the bill and on their way out, they paused by the cash register to watch the final shot of the game as Carolina put Clemson away for the year, 78–66.

Chapter
Nine

All up and down the radio dial, sportscasters were going wild. Duke and Georgia Tech see-sawed back and forth with the lead.

"Duke's ahead 61–59. Here comes Price with a twenty-five-footer. Tech ties it up for the ninth time. Duke in possession. *Stolen* by Petway. Twelve seconds left—Petway to Price—*missed!* And we're going into over-time!" shrieked a hoarse announcer.

Kate kept her eyes on the road, but her fingers continued to twiddle the dial knob until she hit a radio station playing an old Beatles song. Her foot relaxed on the accelerator and she dropped just below the speed limit, soothed as always by the strains of "Penny Lane."

An aroma of celery and freshly baked wheat rolls rose from the brown grocery sacks on the back seat.

"More fruits and vegetables and roughage," the obstetrician had said. The doctor had been brisk and efficient and, on the whole, pleased with Kate's physical condition. "But no nonsense about dieting," she told Kate. "You're almost too thin. Drink a milk shake once in a while and try to cut out the cigarettes."

Dr. Teresa Yates had been recommended by her doctor in New York, and Kate thought they would probably be compatible once basketball season ended. There was a small television set in the waiting room and Dr. Yates's nurse kept popping in and out to relay the score throughout Kate's examination.

It figured. A certificate behind Dr. Yates's desk announced that she had interned at Duke Hospital.

There was one good side to the tournament, though. Kate hated having anyone hover while she tried on clothes, and the salesclerks at the maternity shop could barely be pried away from the game long enough to take her money for the slacks and tops she'd selected and tried on as freely as if she'd been alone in her own closet.

At the crossroads before her turnoff to the farm, Kate pulled in at a shabby white-frame country grocery and parked between a late-model pickup and one that was even older than Lacy's.

Inside, the potbellied stove had been replaced by a small gas grate, but several men still sat around the soft drink chest on upended wooden cartons and slat-bottomed chairs to watch the ball game on a black-and-white television set up in a corner. They gave polite nods as Kate entered.

Cracker barrels and open bins of pickles were long gone and penny candy was two for a nickel these days, yet some things remained as they were when Jake was a small boy and had ridden his bike here for his mother to pick up items not worth a special trip into town: a loaf of bread, cigarettes, a quart of milk, or, best of all, a wedge of cheese.

Wheels of mild cheddar—everyone called it hoop cheese—still came in round wooden boxes, and no city supermarket could match its flavor. Mrs. Fowler, the stout and graying matron who tended the store, rose to fetch her knife as Kate approached the counter.

"Bet I know what you want," she smiled, and Kate acknowledged that she'd guessed correctly.

As the storekeeper cut off a generous hunk, weighed and wrapped it in waxed paper, she told Kate how glad they were to hear she was going to be living here for good; then, lowering her voice, said how awful it was that someone had been killed in her packhouse and did Dwight Bryant have any idea who he was or why he was there?

"Not for sure," said Kate. "I believe they're still checking his fingerprints."

Before she could open her purse, Mrs. Fowler asked, "Want me to put this on y'all's tab?"

"Tab?" asked Kate.

The woman's kindly face took on an embarrassed look. "I thought maybe—that is, uh— Well, did you mean to keep on like Jake did?"

"I'm sorry, Mrs. Fowler, but I don't understand."

"Well, see, Mr. Lacy's always put things on tab here—gas, drinks, Nabs and such little mess as that—and then Jake always paid it 'fore he went back to New York." Like many country people, Mrs. Fowler was self-conscious about appearing to press for payment. "There's no rush," she assured Kate, "but it's starting to be right much and—"

"*How* much?" asked Kate.

Mrs. Fowler consulted a little green notepad that had "Honeycutt" penciled on the front. She punched keys on her old-fashioned adding machine, then tore off the tape and handed it to Kate: $347.63.

"I know that's a lot," Mrs. Fowler apologized, "but it's been five months and I'm sure Mr. Lacy didn't realize . . ."

Kate made herself smile reassuringly. "It's all right. It's just that I don't have my checkbook with me."

"Oh, no hurry," said Mrs. Fowler, anxious to put money talk behind them. "No hurry at all."

Nevertheless, as Kate returned to her car with the cheese, she realized that $347.63 probably represented a full month's profit for Mrs. Fowler. Lacy really shouldn't have let it go so long. On the other hand, if Jake had been automatically taking care of it for him, Lacy had probably forgotten that his day to day out-of-pocket expenses were now his own responsibility. She and Jake had always paid the utilities at the farm and restocked the freezer and pantry when they were down, because Jake said Lacy was too proud to take money. Evidently not too proud to let Jake pay his bills, though.

She approached the cutoff to the road past the Honeycutt farm, and she saw Willy Stewart out on his tractor, an enormous John Deere with a closed-in cab and some sort of wide mechanism trailing along behind.

It inched across the field, axle-deep in lush green oats, and it looked to Kate like some prehistoric brontosaurus munching its way across a herbaceous plain.

She signaled for a right turn just as Miss Emily zoomed up from the opposite direction with her left-turn signal flashing erratically from its electric-purple fender.

Kate waved and started past, but Miss Emily honked her horn and signaled for Kate to roll down her window.

"Stop and visit with me a few minutes," the older woman invited.

"Okay," she called, and Miss Emily whipped in front of her to lead the way through the drive and around to the back.

Since coming to the country, Kate often amused herself by trying to spot houses that actually used their front doors. Often, the front entrances were completely abandoned. They sat in stately isolation facing beautiful lawns unmarked by even a walk to connect doors to the grounds. Most seemed to be used only for home funerals or weddings. Unless a house was as grand as Gilead, or the callers total strangers, everyone came to the back door automatically and passed through the kitchen to more formal areas of the house.

Emily Bryant slung an armload of books and folders onto the deacon's bench inside her glassed-in sunporch.

The orange jacket of her yellow and orange pantsuit followed. Beneath, a fuzzy orange jersey molded her plump torso. She looked like a little round tangerine as she bustled about her kitchen.

"Well, that's *one* week I'm glad to see finished. I had those McNeeley twins in my office four times this week. They're going to spend the rest of the year in detention hall if they don't straighten up their wing feathers and start flying in the same direction as their teachers. Their daddy was just the same but I was twenty years younger when he came through school and there was only one of him. How was Robbie? Was the doctor nice? And wasn't that Duke game the most exciting thing you ever saw?"

Kate laughed. "I didn't see it."

"Well, neither did I," Miss Emily admitted. "Those dratted McNeeleys. But I heard the end of overtime on my way home. Iced tea, or would you rather have a Pepsi with something in it?"

"Tea's fine," said Kate, who no longer saw anything odd about the ubiquitous beverage.

From icy January through sweltering August, few were the true Tar Heels who didn't keep a half-gallon jar of iced tea in the refrigerator year-round. Although most of the towns were wet now, the counties were still predominantly dry, so everyone had grown up on soft drinks or iced tea. Until recently, with or without lemon were the only choices offered. City restaurants had learned to ask before adding sugar, but most crossroads cafes still took for granted that their patrons expected iced tea to arrive at the table strong and sweet.

"But wasn't Christ's first miracle turning water to wine?" Kate had asked when originally confronted with the Bible Belt's official antipathy to anything alcoholic.

"Yeah," Jake had grinned, "but the Southern Baptists' first miracle was turning the wine to iced tea."

Remembering, Kate smiled as she took the tall frosty glass.

Miss Emily smiled back, her plump face rosy beneath the tangled red curls. "Did you hear the baby's heartbeat today?"

Kate paused in mid-sip. "Yes, I did! How did you know? Was that nurse another of Bessie's nieces?"

"Just a guess. Well, no, I do listen to what some of the younger teachers tell me and they get so excited when the doctor puts the stethoscope in their ears. Our doctors never thought to let my generation in on the fun. Whenever people start talking about the good old days, I say let them have it. Can you imagine what childbirth must have been like for my mother? You're not going to have amniocentesis, are you?"

Kate dragged her thoughts away from that miraculous little heartbeat she'd heard today between the sturdier thumps of her own heart. "No, the doctor didn't say anything about needing it. Why?"

"Oh, well, I expect I'm old-fashioned, but it seems like knowing the sex months ahead is like knowing in July what Santa Claus is going to bring you for Christmas. All the mystery's gone."

As she spoke, the back door opened and Bessie Stewart came in with a basket of neatly folded, if bizarrely colored, laundry.

"All what mystery's gone?" she asked. "Dwight find out who that man was in your packhouse, Kate?"

Again, as with Rob earlier, Kate explained about Jake's army friend with a similar mole and how she'd found the pictures this morning and relayed the name to Dwight, who, she regretted to report, was too engrossed with basketball to come out this afternoon.

"But it's the ACC Tournament," said Miss Emily.

"So I've heard," Kate said dryly. "I'm surprised to see Willy out in the field, Bessie. I thought he was a rabid fan, too."

"He's not too partial to Duke," said Bessie. " 'Sides, he's got a radio on the tractor and I 'spect he heard Duke give Georgia a whipping. Don't try to talk to him tonight, though. If State don't beat Maryland, there won't be no living with that man the rest of March."

She shook her head when Emily offered tea and passed on through the kitchen to put away the laundry.

"I guess I'd better be on my way," said Kate, slowly pulling on her jacket.

"Lacy minding his manners any better today?" asked Miss Emily, who seemed to read her shifting mood.

"Some. By the way, who's Tucker Sauls?"

"Tucker Sauls? He runs a little sawmill up past the county line. Why?"

"No reason. He was there when I got back from dinner with Gordon and Mary Pat—and I might have known that was your niece helping with dinner, Bessie," she teased as the other returned.

"It's right nice having her close by," Bessie said guilelessly.

"What about Tucker Sauls?" Miss Emily persisted.

"Not much. He was there and Lacy introduced him. Said they were going to haul some logs out of the bottom for firewood. I just wondered if he was someone I was supposed to remember since Lacy made a point of introducing him."

"I'm surprised you haven't met him before," said Miss Emily. "They're old fishing buddies from way back."

"Had 'em a fish trap down on the creek twenty-five years ago, didn't they?" asked Bessie with an arched eyebrow.

"Needed tending night and day," Miss Emily agreed with solemn impishness.

"What?" asked Kate, who sensed a hidden mirth.

"Nothing, nothing," they chorused.

"Oh, come on," Kate wheedled. "What were they doing? Courting?"

The thought of Lacy Honeycutt and Tucker Sauls sweet-talking any women into joining them at a fish trap set them giggling like teenagers and Kate had a sudden glimpse of the laughter and intimacy these two had shared for over half a century.

"Well," said Miss Emily, "you knew that Lacy used to own land on the other side of the creek towards Dobbs?"

"Yes. Jake said the farm went all the way to the crossroads before his grandfather divided it."

"That's right. Andrew got the homeplace, him being the older; and Lacy got the piece east of Blacksnake Creek. Andrew was always sensible and settled, but Lacy was—"

She hesitated and looked at Bessie.

"Wild," Bessie said promptly.

"Not really mean, though."

"Maybe not polecat-mean," said Bessie, striving for strict fairness, "but you got to say he was the devil's playmate sometimes. Remember that night he got Hassie Ferrell drunk and left him for dead in the gravehole that'd been dug for old Mr. Tink's funeral? And the time Willy's cousin Marcellus—"

"Even dead and skinned, Marcellus should've known the difference between a skunk and a possum," Miss Emily interrupted. "Anyhow, we're talking about Tucker Sauls and that still he and Lacy used to have down on Lacy's side of the creek bottom."

"A still?" asked Kate.

Both women nodded.

"A *moonshine* still?"

"Just a little one," said Bessie, still being fair.

"Couldn't have been very big or they wouldn't have been able to keep moving it up and down the creek bank till Sheriff Enloe got tired of hunting for it," Miss Emily said complacently. "They weren't doing it for money. Just wanted somethimg smooth for themselves and a few friends."

"Would've been all right if they kept it to grown-ups," Bessie chuckled. A gold crown gleamed behind her warm brown lips whenever she laughed.

"They sold white lightning to *children?*"

"Not sold," said Miss Emily. "What happened was, Jake followed Lacy down to the still when he was about four one day and pestered them till Tucker Sauls gave him a little noggin. Men! It was just like them to forget little boys don't have the same constitution as big boys. Jake got drunk as a lord and first he threw up and then he turned green and fell down. Scared the pure mischief out of Lacy and Tucker, too, for once.

"They came trucking up to the house with Jake passed out over Lacy's shoulder and tried to get him up to bed without Jane noticing.

"Miss Jane and Mr. Andrew, they didn't hold with drinking," said Bessie.

"Bessie doesn't either," Miss Emily confided. "She thinks I'm going straight to hell because of that bottle of Dickle I keep under the sink."

"I don't either say you're going straight to hell," said Bessie. "I just say you're going to have some tall explaining to do, that's all."

"Anyhow, Andrew didn't approve, but he'd sort of turned a blind eye to Lacy's way 'cause they were brothers," said Miss Emily. "Jane found out, of course, and sailed into all three of 'em and Andrew took his ax to the still and the fish trap, too."

"I never heard that story," Kate laughed.

"Remember the time them two had old Mr. Lavelle Barbour thinking it was Sam Fisher stealing his watermelons?" asked Bessie.

"And the night they put Amos Kornegay's prize hound in his henhouse so he'd think it'd turned into an eggsucker?"

They told a few more stories of Lacy's younger days and his practical jokes and heavy rural humor; but when Kate was gone, Miss Emily looked at Bessie and neither needed speech to know that the other also remembered darker things they had not told Kate.

"Wonder what them two old scoundrels are up to now?" asked Bessie.

Chapter Ten

The object of their mirth and speculation was absent from the house when Kate returned and there was no sign of his fourteen-year-old pickup nor of the dogs.

Kate put away the groceries, changed into jeans and a double layer of loose sweaters since the afternoon was still cool, then rummaged through her cartons until she found a sketchpad and her case of drawing colors.

That morning, she had noticed a cluster of bluets in the grass beside the old well and she carried her pad and pens out, found an old bucket which she upturned for a stool, and began to draw.

Bluets, Quaker-ladies, *Houstonia caerulea*. By any of its names, the minute blue flower held a special charm for Kate. The flat, four-petaled flowers were seldom more than half an inch across and grew on slender stems only three or four inches tall. Alone, they went almost unnoticed, but when found in large colonies, the effect was like wisps of blue lace dropped carelessly upon the grass.

Size and depth of color could vary. Kate had seen some so pale that they were almost white; in others, the blue echoed a spring sky. These that she had discovered were very tiny and of a rich blue that was almost purple. Instead of the usual yellow, they had deep reddish-blue eyes.

She filled a sheet of her sketchpad with careful, exact details, and the colors of her fine-tipped felt pens were as vibrant as the bluets themselves.

Absorbed in recreating the image of stem, leaf, and minute seedpod, Kate had barely noticed the sound of a chain saw from the woods below the wide fields; but gradually, she realized it had to be Lacy working down there in dogged solitude.

Gordon Tyrrell's reminder of how Jake's death must have devastated Lacy, followed by Bessie and Miss Emily's recital of the old man's younger, mischief-loving days nibbled at Kate's conscience. Whether Lacy would admit it or not, each was all the other had left of Jake right now, and shouldn't youth defer to age?

She dug up a pair of old gardening gloves and set off down the slope, following the chain saw's high shriek.

The woods were a mixture of deciduous trees and pines. Maples and elms were beginning to flower, oaks were still bare. Along the edge of the field, every sassafras twig was precisely tipped with a single greenish-yellow flower, each so stiffly stylized that Kate wondered if they'd come down unchanged from the Triassic.

Beyond the curve of the woodline, she found Lacy cutting off tree limbs with an agility to belie his seventy-odd years. He maneuvered the heavy raucous saw with practiced deliberation, separating limbs from trunk until the recently felled tree was reduced to an unencumbered log. She watched him cut the thicker limbs into stove-sized pieces and he didn't notice her presence until the three dogs circled past to greet her. Distracted by their rush, Lacy eased off on the saw's throttle and looked around warily.

Kate picked her way through the brushy limbs until

she was near enough to shout above the motor, "Can I help you? Load wood or something?"

He shut off the saw to hear.

"I'm sorry," said Kate. "I didn't mean to slow you down. I just wondered if there was something I could do to help."

To her relief, instead of growling a refusal, Lacy looked at her dubiously. "You reckon you ought to strain yourself?" he asked with rough delicacy.

"A little exercise will be good for me," she assured him.

"Well," he said, looking at the fallen debris, "it'd be a help to have the brush piled."

He dragged a limb past his rusty old pickup and out into the edge of the field. "Ought to be safe to burn it out here."

"Burn?"

"These here trees has got the borer beetle in 'em," said Lacy. "We don't get 'em out and burn the brush, they'll keep spreading all through these woods."

He pulled back the pine bark and exposed the runnels where borers had channeled beneath and eaten into the soft cambium layer. Two or three nearby trees showed telltale symptoms of distress by their brown needles.

"Is it bad?" asked Kate, who knew nothing about forest pests. "Can anything be done to stop them?"

"I'm a-doing it!" Lacy said with a flare of his former testiness.

As if he'd heard the shortness in his tone, Kate could actually see him make an effort to tolerate her ignorance.

"See, they don't hardly mess with healthy trees. Just young ones or ones that already has something wrong with 'em. If I cull out all the ones where they've started and burn all the laps, it ought to keep 'em down."

"Except for those three trees, the rest are pretty healthy, aren't they?" Kate asked hopefully.

Lacy carefully extinguished the cigarette that dangled from the corner of his mouth and looked around the woods with a negative roll of his head. "About a tenth of the pines and maybe even a few hardwoods'll have to come out."

He gestured toward a tall pine whose needles were thick and green yet. "See that sawdust? That's borer beetles."

Kate went closer and saw white powdery streaks that had spilled down along the trunk from small holes in the rough brown bark. A tenth of the pines! "Can you manage it alone?"

"Tucker Sauls said he'd go shares. Where the wood's still sound, he can saw 'em into boards. The rest we'll use for firewood."

The old man hesitated and fumbled with the chain saw, his eyes not meeting hers. "That's if it's all right with you."

Kate suddenly realized that he was embarrassed, that he was asking her permission because she owned the land now and could veto decisions he'd always made freely before. It was her turn to feel embarrassed.

"Whatever you want to do is fine with me, Lacy. You know more about what a farm needs than I ever will."

He nodded and abruptly pulled the starter of the gasoline-powered chain saw. It roared to life in a cloud of blue smoke and Lacy returned to work.

Hoping she'd said the right thing, Kate began dragging the unwanted limbs out to the edge of the field. By sunset, Lacy had felled two more trees and her brush pile was head-high and several yards across.

"It'll make a right good-size bonfire," said Lacy as she left to start supper.

By eight P.M. Kate had reached a lazy halfway point: she knew she should go to bed, yet she lacked the energy to move. There was a pleasant tiredness in her arms from the unaccustomed labor, the fire Lacy had built in the kitchen range made the room just a little too cozy, and it was lovely to lie somnolently on the wide leather couch and let the television act as a soporific.

Young men raced up and down with a basketball; crafty coaches worked the referees; and, during time-outs, someone in a turtle suit turned cartwheels across the polished hardwood while a raffish wolf led a group of red-clad cheerleaders at the near end of the court. From the depths of his recliner chair, Lacy snorted everytime a call went against N.C. State and sneered, "It's about time those damnfools caught him," whenever a Maryland player was charged with a foul.

Kate could not appreciate the finer nuances of the game, but since State had trailed the whole first half, sometimes by as much as eight points, she rather doubted there was going to be much joy in Mudville tonight.

"Poor Bessie," she thought, and settled her head a little more comfortably into the pillow.

A moment after the halftime buzzer sounded, the telephone rang.

"Probably for you this time of night," said Lacy, unmoving.

Kate struggled to her feet. "Just as well. If I don't stir, I'm going to fall asleep."

The cooler air out in the hall helped clear her muzzy head, but she had to stifle a yawn to answer.

"Kate?" said Gordon Tyrrell. "Did I wake you?"

"In about three more minutes, I would have said yes, but you caught me just in time."

"Good. Listen, Kate, has Dwight Bryant called?"

"No. Was he supposed to? Lacy and I were both out until almost dark this afternoon. Why?"

"It's the damnedest thing. I went up to the attic today to look for James's trunk and somebody's already been through it."

"What do you mean?"

"I mean, somebody's wrenched the lock off its hasp, pawed through James's things and taken all his Vietnam stuff!"

"That's weird. When do you think it happened?"

"Bryant asked me that when I phoned to tell him I wouldn't be able to help with a sharper picture of Covington. It can't have been recently because there was a layer of dust all over the trunk. We've all used the attic as a storage bin and I think James dropped it off here early last spring. He'd just given up his apartment in Washington and Elaine and I met him here and then we all flew out to Vail for the last of the skiing."

"That's almost a year," said Kate. "Didn't the caretaker notice if the house had been broken into?"

"I've tried to call Rob Bryant to ask if he knows anything, but he doesn't answer his phone. I wondered if perhaps something happened while I was in the hospital—something they told me and I was too groggy to remember? The Whitleys have been here since September though, and neither of them knew of any breakins, so it must have happened sometime between Easter and Labor Day."

"Was anything else taken?"

"Not that we can tell. The maid says all the silver seems to be intact and so far as I can remember there aren't any pictures missing; but Rob Bryant has the inventory records and we'll have to wait until he can bring them out to be sure."

"What did Dwight say?"

"He suggests that we not touch anything," Gordon said dryly. "I think he's seen too many old movies. I had to tell him I'd already handled everything and so had the help because I called them up to ask if they'd noticed the broken lock earlier."

"Had they?"

"They say not. The cook and maids say they were never in the attic at all and Tom Whitley said the only time he and Sally were up was when they put their luggage there in September and ours in December. Anyhow, Bryant—Dwight Bryant—seems to think the picture of Covington's become important, and he wanted to let you know he'd be out at eight-thirty tomorrow to get yours."

Kate thanked him for relaying the message and they talked a few minutes longer, wondering if the theft were a coincidence or somehow connected to the later murder.

When Kate returned to the warm kitchen, Lacy was sitting at the table in his stocking feet with a big glass of milk and a slice of the cherry cheesecake Kate had picked up for their dessert in Raleigh that afternoon. Lacy had a weakness for sweets, but almost never bought any for himself.

He wasn't very interested in Gordon's discovery. "James probably lost the key and busted it open hisself before they went down to Mexico," he said, his attention focused on the television.

It was still halftime and a commercial showed an earnest farm agent extolling the benefits of a certain broadleaf herbicide for higher corn yields. He was followed by singing termites routed by clouds of bug spray.

Thus reminded, Kate paused by the corner bookshelf and carried an illustrated book of insect pests back to the couch with her.

There were three pages of different borers and each seemed evolved for a specific tree. Among evergreen pests were listed Douglas fir beetles, spruce beetles, birch borers, western pine beetles and southern pine beetles. The book, printed before Rachel Carson's *Silent Spring*, laconically suggested that most pests could be controlled with contact pesticides, beginning with DDT and ending with parathion.

Kate continued to turn pages past ticks and lice, harlequin beetles and cutworms. Aesthetically, some of the pests were colorful and strikingly marked. She could almost adapt some of the designs for fabrics. But after browsing through lurid descriptions of their destructive force, Kate wound up feeling somewhat paranoid. Every flower, shrub and tree; every domestic animal from cows and sheep to geese and chickens had its own species-specific parasite or bloodsucker.

There was a reason people sometimes let pesticides get out of hand, she decided.

• • •

Maryland and State had rejoined the battle and Kate put the book aside. As those sweaty young players leaped and dribbled and performed incredible feats with the ball, her eyelids grew heavy and soon she slept.

Chapter Eleven

The coffee had finished perking and the unmistakable smell of salt-cured country ham hung over the kitchen. Kate found her appetite growing as she unfolded her napkin and waited for Lacy to fill her plate with fluffy scrambled eggs and a healthy dollop of grits.

The milk and butter were supermarket staples, but the eggs were from Lacy's Rhode Island Reds and Bessie Stewart had sent over a pint jar of cherry preserves.

"Umm!" Kate sighed as Lacy ladled a spoonful of red-eye gravy over the grits.

"Thought you didn't like breakfast," said Lacy. His tone was crusty as ever, but he looked pleased when Kate helped herself to a large piece of ham from the platter.

"It's my favorite meal," said Kate, forgetful of those mornings she'd diplomatically stayed in bed so that Lacy could talk with Jake more freely. "Especially down here."

She cut a bite of the leathery ham and savored its strong salty flavor. "The nice thing about North Carolina ham is the way it doesn't melt in your mouth. Did you cure this one? The flavor's wonderful."

"Take a biscuit while it's hot," said Lacy, embarrassed by her praise. "They ain't fit to eat once they get cold."

The old farmer had a light hand with eggs, but he'd never caught the knack for hot breads. When canned biscuits came on the market, he'd gratefully retired his rolling pin.

Since last evening, the silences between them had begun to feel more natural and less strained. The breakfast wouldn't take a prize for scintillating conversation, but at least Lacy was sociable enough this morning to talk about cooking problems as they ate. He reached for a final biscuit even though they were cool by then.

"My mammy used to make biscuits that held their taste stone cold and twelve hours old. We'd wrap 'em round a piece of sausage and carry 'em down to the fish trap and they'd taste just as good at midnight as they did that morning. But these puny things—"

The telephone trilled and Lacy stepped down the hall to answer. "Some man for you," he said. "Says he's calling from New York."

Puzzled, Kate took the phone.

"Darling Katherine!" exclaimed a deep male voice. "I'm missing you like crazy. When are you coming back to civilization?"

Richard Cromyn was Gina Melnick's assistant and Kate's longtime friend. For years they had carried on the bantering fiction that passion simmered just below the surface of their friendship and that, were it not for her Jake and Richard's Donald, they would have eloped to Tahiti ages ago.

"I'm longing for you, too, darling," Kate said throatily, "but we must remain firm to our resolve."

Richard's tone turned serious. "Are you sure it isn't too awful down there without Jake?"

"In some ways," she admitted, "but I still want to have our baby here."

"Brave Katherine! Listen, lovey, Gina's here. She wants to bully you about the Astin repeats. Donald sends his love and so do I."

"I love you, too, Richard," Kate smiled as he turned the line over to Gina, who thought hard work a good antidote for grief and loneliness. She made Kate promise to complete the Astin project that week.

As Kate replaced the receiver and reentered the kitchen, the dogs began barking and she looked through the west windows to see Dwight Bryant's unmarked patrol car pull in from the lane.

"Looks like that deputy's brought the sheriff out with him," Lacy scowled.

He pushed back from the table and went out to meet them. Kate felt a rush of chill morning air as the door opened and closed, even though the sun was bright outside. She continued with her breakfast, knowing the men had a certain amount of ritual to get through before anything pertinent could get said. They would probably talk about the weather, the condition of the fields, the prospects of setting out tobacco on time; then basketball ought to be good for another three minutes since few Colleton County citizens would be happy with State's loss to Maryland last night.

"Well, at least Wake Forest licked Virginia," said Lacy, and led the other two men in just as Kate swallowed the last morsel of ham on her plate.

"Don't let us stop your breakfast," said Dwight when Kate rose.

"I've just finished. All except for another cup of coffee. Don't you want some?"

She included the third man in her question and the big detective hastened to introduce them. "Kate Honeycutt, this is Sheriff Poole."

Bowman Poole, Bo to his friends, appeared to be in his late fifties. His hair was the yellow of sunbleached broom straw and beginning to thin, his long face was pleasantly creased, and there were laugh lines around his blue eyes. Those penetrating eyes were on the same level as hers Kate noticed as he gave a firm handshake, and he seemed quite fit except for a small paunch that tightened the vest buttons of his three-piece brown suit.

"No coffee for us, ma'am," he said, "but you go right ahead with yours."

"I know you want to see those pictures," Kate said, as they sat. "They're just down the hall."

But when she reached the cluttered front parlor, she had to pause and get her bearings. There were the boxes and cartons she'd opened yesterday and there was the one on which she thought she'd left the manila envelope. For a moment, Kate wondered if she'd taken the envelope to her room, but then she remembered that after Gordon Tyrrell and Tom Whitley left yesterday, she'd gone straight out to the clothesline and then to her room to change. She tried to recall if she'd seen it when she was rummaging for pad and drawing pens to sketch the bluets. Nothing came to mind.

Puzzled, she returned to the kitchen and, without thinking how it would sound, said, "Lacy, did you take that envelope of Jake's?"

She saw his jaw tighten and quickly added, "For safekeeping, I mean?"

It was too late.

"I ain't been near your things," Lacy said stiffly.

He began to clear the table, spooning all the scraps and leftovers into the egg bowl for the dogs. His bony face had closed down and his manner made it clear to the others that his socializing was over.

"I'm sorry," Kate told Poole and Dwight helplessly. "I thought I left the envelope on top of an open carton yesterday afternoon, but it's not there now."

"Mind if we take a look?" asked Sheriff Poole. "Maybe it blew off or slid down behind something."

Rob arrived while they searched and he was in time to hear Kate repeat her description of the previous morning and how Tom Whitley had cut open the carton and Gordon Tyrrell had helped spot the right snapshot of the Vietnam foursome.

"So after you called Dwight here and told him Covington's name, you put the picture back in the envelope and just left it on this box?" asked Poole.

Kate nodded.

"Then, as I understand it, you went to Raleigh?"

Again she nodded.

Poole turned to Lacy. "What about you, Mr. Lacy?"

"I watched Carolina beat Clemson out yonder in the kitchen and then cut wood till suppertime."

"Don't suppose you locked the house before you left?"

"Never felt no need to," said Lacy. "Nothing here worth taking."

"I can vouch for the door being unlocked," said Rob.

Kate looked at him in surprise.

"I stopped by on my way to Dobbs late in the afternoon," he explained. "You dropped your lipstick in my car yesterday and I wanted to return it. Your car was here, but when I knocked and no one answered, I stuck my head in the door and called."

He handed Kate a small black enamel tube. Kate twirled it open. Tahiti Twilight, a deep plummy red.

"Sorry," she said. "It's not mine. From the color, I'd say a very sexy brunette."

"Fast company," said Dwight.

Rob pocketed the lipstick with a slight flush on his triangular face.

"I hate to impose on you folks," said the sheriff, "but if you don't mind, Mrs. Honeycutt, Mr. Lacy, I'd like to phone Mr. Tyrrell and get him and that caretaker of his over here."

Kate agreed and they returned to the kitchen.

While they waited for Gordon and Tom Whitley, Dwight told them that the Wheeler boy had helped narrow down the time of death. "He works the late shift in Raleigh and was coming home through the lane a little past one-thirty early Thursday morning. He says there was a dark, late-model car—he thinks it was a Chevrolet—pulled in beside the packhouse, out of sight of your house and off the lane. He didn't recognize the car and he can't say if anyone was in it, but he didn't think twice about it. Wednesday night's still a dating night and it's not the first time he's passed a car parked there."

"Well, it certainly wasn't there at midnight when I drove past," said Kate. "I'm sure I would have noticed."

"So sometime between midnight and four o'clock," Rob mused.

"With Willy's dogs barking in that direction until almost twelve-thirty, according to Willy," said his brother.

"Did you hear from Washington yet?" Kate asked. "Was it really Bernie Covington?"

"It was," said Poole. "We got more than just an ID, too. Covington had a dishonorable discharge from the army in 1972, drug trafficking. He was born in California and pulled some time there for assault with a deadly weapon. Last year, he skipped bail in Florida for drugs again. Nothing on his whereabouts since then. Reckon he's been laying low."

There was a light knock at the door and Emily Bryant bounced into the kitchen, fresh from the local beauty parlor, with her newly-retouched auburn curls as bright as the morning sun behind her.

"Well, for heaven's sake!" she cried. "Look who-all's here. I saw Rob's car, but I didn't know anybody was with you, Dwight. How are you, Bo? Haven't seen you since last Mule Day. I can tell Marnie's cooking still agrees with you, though. Kate, honey, I keep forgetting to give you this pie Bessie baked for you, so I thought I'd run over with it and see if Lacy'd pour me a cup of his good coffee.

"I'm not interrupting anything, am I?" she asked with wide-eyed innocence, and before they could answer, she had pulled a chair up to the table between Rob and Dwight and was beaming at them happily.

Lacy snorted, Dwight and Rob looked resigned, but Bo Poole smiled back at her affectionately. "You sure you didn't come over to tell me who killed that man

Wednesday night?" he teased. "You must be getting old, Miss Em'ly."

"Don't you get sassy with me," she warned. "This is an election year and you've got a tough row to hoe up here in this end of the county."

Bo Poole possessed a folksy, good-old-boy courtliness, and Kate enjoyed his banter with Miss Emily, a teasing familiarity of place and style that had carried the county every election day since he first chose to run.

From where she sat, Emily Bryant had a clear view of the yard through the windows behind Poole. "Now who's this coming? Gordon? Gordon Tyrrell and Tom Whitley. My goodness, Bo, you *are* having a get-together, aren't you? Good thing I dropped in, Kate. All these men and just you."

The sunny kitchen became a bit crowded as Tyrrell and Whitley joined them. Gordon shook hands easily with the sheriff and Rob Bryant, nodded to Lacy and Dwight, and greeted Kate and Miss Emily; but Tom Whitley hung back shyly and when Kate tried to offer him a chair at the big round table, he ducked his head and allowed as how he'd been sitting all morning and would just as soon lean against the counter for a change.

Kate gathered that Rob had already spoken to Gordon that morning, for she heard Rob tell him that he'd brought a copy of Gilead's inventory.

Sheriff Poole waited until the amenities were over and those who wanted coffee or cigarettes were provided with cups and ashtrays. He was not the tallest man there, yet when he settled back in his chair and cleared his throat, he conveyed considerable authority. The folksy ease did not disappear, but even Miss Emily quit talking and looked at him expectantly.

"I asked y'all to come over, Mr. Tyrrell, because Mrs. Honeycutt tells me you and Mr. Whitley were here yesterday when she unpacked the pictures of her husband and your brother from their army days."

"That's right," said Gordon. "Detective Bryant had

phoned to ask if she'd found the name of the man who served with James and Jake. I didn't see the dead man Thursday, but Kate thought he looked like this Covington. What do you think?"

"Well, we know it's Covington," said Poole. "Washington's identified his fingerprints and they're going to mail us a picture even though it seems like somebody doesn't want Detective Bryant or me looking at it too quick. Sometime after you people saw it yesterday, that envelope of Jake Honeycutt's war stuff turned up missing."

"Missing?" asked Gordon.

"Missing or stolen?" asked Miss Emily.

"Like James's things?" wondered Gordon. "But that's so futile. Why would someone bother to take those pictures? Surely they would know Covington could be identified as soon as you compared fingerprints."

He frowned at Poole apprehensively. "His fingertips weren't mutilated, were they?"

Miss Emily blanched, but Bo Poole disabused them of that idea. "No, nothing like that. There has to be a reason though. That's what I wanted to ask you and Mr. Whitley—was there anything about the pictures that struck you odd?"

"I hardly saw them," Tom Whitley blurted from his stand at the counter. "I was already out of the room before Mrs. Honeycutt put everything back in that envelope and I didn't go back in."

"Easy, Tom," said Gordon Tyrrell. "No one's accusing you of taking it."

Whitley's deep-set eyes shifted over the group. His face was wary and his body tense. Kate sympathized, knowing how it felt to be an outsider.

"It isn't just pictures," she reminded Sheriff Poole. "That envelope held Jake's Purple Heart and souvenirs he picked up in Vietnam."

She turned to Gordon. "Was anything missing from James's trunk besides the pictures?"

"There was a little cedar chest," said Gordon. "As

clearly as I can recall, it held the same sort of things there were in Jake's envelope—not just pictures, but some letters, traveling papers, and other odds and ends. The chest is gone and everything in it."

"What about you, Mr. Lacy?" asked Poole. "Detective Bryant tells me you lost some pictures, too. Was there anything else?"

"Just them pictures Jake sent me."

"Okay," said Poole. "Now y'all stop me if I get any of this wrong, but the way I understand it is that Jake Honeycutt, James Tyrrell, this Bernie Covington, and a young man they called Kid met up together in Vietnam, right?"

"They was on patrol together," said Lacy.

"And just by happenstance," added Kate. "James and Jake met in basic training and they didn't really know the other two until that dreadful patrol."

"They got separated and everybody with them was killed except those four, right?" asked Poole.

Kate, Gordon, and Lacy nodded.

"Then a sniper tried to shoot Jake, but your brother and this Covington killed him first and later they camped in an old ruined temple where they almost bumped into a Vietcong patrol?"

"That's what Jake writ me," agreed Lacy.

"And so far as you know, Jake Honeycutt and James Tyrrell had nothing to do with Covington or the fourth man after Vietnam?"

Troubled, Kate murmured her agreement with the others but she began to see what Sheriff Poole was driving at.

"But they *are* connected, aren't they, Sheriff? James is dead, Jake is dead, and now Bernie Covington. Oh, God!" she cried as the full meaning broke upon her.

"It *wasn't* an accident, was it?"

Chapter Twelve

Through the babble of voices, Kate pinned Lacy's eyes with her own blazing glance.

"Jake always swore he was careful with guns," she said. "Why did you let them call it an accident?"

The old man glared back at her and a muscle twitched in his bony jaw. "I fetched the law out 'fore I moved him, didn't I?"

"Now let's not everybody get excited," Sheriff Poole soothed diplomatically.

"They didn't take anything for granted, Kate," said Dwight. "I looked up the file this morning and talked to the detectives who worked the case. They treated it like any unexplained death: took pictures, fingerprinted the gun, searched the whole area inch by inch. Jake was tangled up in the barbed wire; his gun was right where he would have dropped it. No scuffling of the pine straw like there'd have been if he'd fought with someone and besides, he didn't have a single mark of any fight—no bruises, no cuts on the back of his hands where he might have hit anybody. Or been hit for that matter."

"Then how—"

"We can't say," said Poole. "For all we know, it might still be a real accident. Except now, you see, we look at your husband gone, Mr. Tyrrell's brother dead, and with this Covington man murdered, well, we've got to wonder."

He turned to Gordon. "Mr. Tyrrell, I never rightly got all the details about your boat accident down in Mexico. Was there a typhoon or did the engine explode or what?"

"It was a storm," Gordon said, his voice hesitant.

"But you don't remember!" Kate exclaimed. "You had a concussion and when you came to, you didn't remember anything at all about that day."

"I didn't, but Mrs. McDermott did," he reminded her. "And one of the crewmen. Both said a sudden squall came up, the main mast snapped, and the boat broke apart."

"They ever find the pieces?" asked Poole.

Gordon shook his head.

Dwight looked gratified. "So you can't swear somebody didn't weaken the mast ahead of time or maybe monkey with some of the equipment so that everything'd fly apart as soon as they had to take any extra strain?"

"No, of course not," said Gordon. "But that's all so iffy."

"Law work mostly is till we get all the facts," said Poole.

"Far as that goes," offered Miss Emily, "three men out of four getting themselves killed is sort of iffy, too."

"Mother," said Rob.

She ignored him. "Makes you sort of wonder where that Kid is, doesn't it?"

"We've asked the army about him," Poole acknowledged. "Won't hurt to know if he's alive and well somewhere in Utah, say."

"Instead of skulking around here, stealing back all

the pictures of himself so we won't know what he looks like?" Gordon suggested thoughtfully.

"There's that possibility," Poole agreed. "Dwight?"

The younger law officer shifted his bulky frame self-consciously. "This is more iffiness, Kate, Mr. Tyrrell, Mr. Lacy, but I hope you'll hear me out. Like Sheriff Poole here says, we have to wonder when we hear that four men served together fifteen years or so ago and now at least three of them are dead within six months of each other. That drowning and Jake's shooting—they look like pure and simple accidents; but what happened to Bernie Covington early Thursday morning was no accident. Somebody smashed his head in and threw him down the packhouse steps."

While Dwight spoke, Kate glanced around the wide table. Gordon and Lacy were engrossed in the detective's words and Miss Emily seemed to be enjoying this inside look at her older son's work. Rob's pointed face was blank as he stared into his coffee cup. She felt Tom Whitley's eyes upon her, yet when she looked toward him, he quickly shied away. Sheriff Poole gazed at them all with a genial expression that didn't quite mask his watchful air.

"—so we know Covington was a crook," Dwight was saying. "Mixed up in drugs, trained in jungle fighting, apt to get violent. A man like that wouldn't think twice about killing. Now what if he and that younger man teamed up to get rid of James and Jake because of something that happened on that patrol?"

"Jake wouldn't have kept something like that a secret," Kate protested.

"Maybe it was something he knew without knowing he knew. Or else—Mr. Lacy, you said Jake told you those four had to camp all night in a temple or something with Vietcong soldiers swarming all around?"

"That's right," said Lacy.

"Well, maybe they found something valuable that night, a gold idol or something they couldn't take with them then so they buried it, planning to go back after the war."

Rob tried not to grin and Gordon snorted. "Shades of Jungle Jim! Next you'll tell us they stole the ruby eye out of a giant Buddha and now, fifteen years later, the ancient curse is finally catching up with them."

Dwight's rugged face turned a dull red.

"But there was a map," Kate said unwillingly. "Remember, Gordon? Part of an army terrain map that had been torn out of a larger map."

Gordon's derisive smile faded and he twisted in his chair to face her. "I *do* remember. James had something like that, too. Do you suppose—?"

Common sense reclaimed him. "No, it really is too preposterous. If James and Jake had shared a secret like that—"

"They didn't realize!" exclaimed Miss Emily, who loved thriller adventure movies and was enchanted by the idea of hidden gold or jewels or foreign idols. "Say Jake and James didn't know about the treasure but they each kept a map, or maybe half a map, of where that temple was located. Say Covington and that other soldier were the two who actually found and stashed the treasure. And when they couldn't find it again after the war, why wouldn't they come looking for the maps they knew James and Jake had kept?"

"Oh come on, Mother!" laughed Rob. "This isn't *Raiders of the Lost Ark.*"

"It could be," she said stubbornly. "Why else would Covington be murdered? He and his friend probably killed James and Jake and stole the maps and pictures and then had a falling out. I'll bet you that other man's on his way back to Vietnam right now with both halves of the map to guide him to the treasure."

Her plump little face was so earnest under its fluffy mobcap of improbably red curls that Rob reached across the table and patted her hand. She snatched it away indignantly. "Such things have happened, Bo," she insisted.

"Maybe," the sheriff conceded, "but I never heard of such in Colleton County. Course, times are changing," he added, remembering some of the bizarre cases that had popped up in the last three or four years as more and more strangers moved into the county. He still found it difficult to pronounce the word "transvestism" and he'd never even heard of "sexual asphyxiation" until the most sophisticated of his detectives reclassified as accidental a death that the coroner originally called a suicide last year.

Hidden Buddhist idols, torn treasure maps, and murders disguised as accidents seemed only marginally more outlandish.

"We'll have to wait and see what the army gives us," he said. "In the meantime, Mr. Tyrrell, how about you tell us the name of that place in Mexico y'all were staying at so Dwight can see if they've learned anything new about that boat since Christmas."

"If you want to stop by Gilead," said Gordon, "I think I may even have the telephone number of the Costa Verde police prefect."

"Fine," said the sheriff. "And Dwight can show me the packhouse on the way over, if that's all right, Mr. Lacy?"

"It's *hers*," Lacy said stonily. "And I've got work to do."

"I'll ride over, too, Gordon," said Rob. "I ought to check the big pieces of silver against the inventory, if nothing else."

The sunny kitchen was abruptly emptied of men.

Kate gathered up cups and saucers, stray spoons and ashtrays, and carried them to the sink of soapy water. Miss Emily automatically flapped open a dish towel and began drying the glassware, but tactful silence was not her strongest point and soon her worried eyes peered up to Kate's.

"Does this make it worse, honey?" she asked.

Kate rinsed a saucer mechanically and set it in the drain rack.

"What do you mean?"

"Is it worse knowing somebody might have killed Jake deliberately?"

Kate stared at her with a welling impatience. Had

Miss Emily been widowed so long she had forgotten the searing pain, the ache of missing someone more dear than—

"At least now you know it wasn't Jake's fault," said Miss Emily, busy with the dish towel; and the truth of her observation sliced open the knots that had constricted Kate ever since that October Sunday.

With the possibility of murder came a realization of what grief had done to her. She had blamed Jake for his own death, for deserting her when she loved him so desperately. But what if it wasn't *his* carelessness? If he hadn't gone by his own actions? What if someone else had taken him from her?

Miss Emily was right. Somehow that would make it a little easier.

Chapter Thirteen

As an adventurous child visiting her Aunt Bessie, DeWanda Sanders had often sneaked over to Gilead and explored its vast decayed emptiness. She had watched Gilead's restoration with interest after Patricia and Philip Carmichael bought it from old Mr. Franklin Gilbert and as a teenager, she had often helped out at big parties or when the house overflowed with guests; therefore she knew more about Gilead's ornaments and furnishings than the rest of the current staff.

While Gordon Tyrrell took the sheriff and Dwight Bryant up to the third floor attic to examine the burgled trunk, DeWanda accompanied Rob Bryant through Gilead's beautiful rooms. The russet-haired lawyer scanned the inventory sheets, reading aloud the most valuable of each room's bibelots, and the young black maid either pointed it out or told him its current location.

She knew that the glass-domed 1847 skeleton clock had been sent to a clockmaker in Atlanta for regulating and that the study's jasper cigarette box was presently in Gordon's private sitting room. In the butler's pantry, she was able to confirm that every silver bowl, goblet, or serving piece was in its proper slot.

To Mary Pat, the adults seemed to be playing games, part treasure hunt, part hide-and-seek. She scampered up and down the wide staircase, now up in the attic with its mysterious boxes and trunks, now down in the drawing room tugging on Rob's hand to come see how she'd put the shepherdess on the mantle in her bedroom so it could keep Jemima Puddle-Duck and Princess Leia company.

Indulging her, for it made no difference to him in which order he took the rooms, Rob followed Mary Pat upstairs and along the hall.

"Hey," said DeWanda. "You're going the wrong way, honey."

But Mary Pat raced to throw open the door of a small guestroom. "This is my really truly room," she said. "This is my bed and that's my chair."

"And where're your clothes and all your pretty toys," laughed DeWanda, who thought Mary Pat was teasing.

"Somebody put them down yonder," said Mary Pat, her solemn little face troubled. "But this is my *real* room."

Rob hesitated. He recognized that this was another manifestation of the child's strange insistence that places and things could change irrationally and arbitrarily, but he wasn't certain whether one was supposed to humor her and agree, or try to reason her out of it.

DeWanda had caught on, too, and her dark eyes melted in concern.

"This is a real nice room, honey," she said, "but your other room's pretty, too, and didn't you want to show Mr. Rob your china dolls?"

Mary Pat was immediately diverted. Chattering of Jemima, Princess Leia, and Princess Georgiana, she willingly skipped along between Rob and DeWanda down to the room that had been hers from birth.

Princess Leia was, of course, a plastic *Star Wars*

toy sold by the millions, the Beatrix Potter figurine was modern porcelain, "Princess Georgiana," a Royal Doulton antique. Mary Pat loved them equally and gave Rob a scornful look when he suggested that she should be extra careful with the shepherdess.

"Manners, Mary Pat," Sally Whitley reminded with a gentle smile.

That young woman had been sorting through Mary Pat's winter wardrobe when the three entered the room, and she paused with a little fur-trimmed parka in her hands while Rob explained their errand.

Sally Whitley had small delicate bones and an old-fashioned prettiness. She wore a blue denim shirtwaist with white cuffs and collar. The severely cut dress was a size too large and, instead of lending maturity, made her look like a teenager playing schoolteacher. Her fair hair was very fine and wisped into natural ringlets around a thin face. A slight overbite gave her a tremulous, vulnerable look. She was naturally shy and her wide hazel eyes usually dropped first if challenged by the eyes of a more assertive person. She reminded Rob of an easily startled woods creature, a young wild rabbit perhaps, timorous and ready to bolt at the first sign of danger.

"I'm sure there's nothing missing here," she told Rob.

Mary Pat's quarters consisted of a large corner bedroom, a playroom and a modern bath. Patricia had chosen bright furnishings for the nursery and, except for a low Martha Washington rocker, everything was contemporary with practical, washable surfaces. The only real item of value was a gold-trimmed mother-of-pearl comb and brush set Philip Carmichael had impulsively bought in a London antique store when Mary Pat was six weeks old.

"It's just a pro forma exercise," said Rob, ticking the dresser set off his inventory. "Whoever broke into the attic probably did it before you and your husband moved in and it doesn't look like they were interested in anything but James Tyrrell's trunk."

"His war souvenirs," Sally nodded. "It seems so odd. To take pictures and papers when this house is full of expensive things."

"It's on account of that dead man," DeWanda said knowingly. "Sheriff Bo's up looking in the attic right now, but he said he wanted to talk to all of us before he left."

"The sheriff?" An expression of alarm flitted across Sally Whitley's face.

"It's only another formality," Rob soothed. "He'll want to know if you-all saw any strangers in the neighborhood last week. There may have been a second man."

"He was under draft age back then, so he'd probably be in his late twenties or early thirties by now," said Dwight Bryant. "We don't have a picture of him yet or any description, but Covington—the dead man—had black hair and that black mole on his right cheek; so two strangers together, with Yankee accents probably, should have been noticed."

The room in which they'd gathered served as both dining and daytime sitting room for the staff. The Whitleys' quarters were on the other side of the kitchen (an intercom connected their room to Mary Pat's almost directly overhead), and the cook and two maids commuted from nearby towns.

"Yankees aren't that noticeable anymore," complained Mrs. Faircloth, a fiftyish woman whose beanbag figure betrayed a fondness for her own cooking. "I remember when I was little and Sam Carroll came to church the first time with his brand-new Philadelphia wife. I never heard such pretty talk in all my born days and I followed her around all afternoon and even stood on the pew bench behind her to hear if she sang her words like she talked them; but nowadays, shootfire! With television and so many strangers moving in, I wouldn't turn around twice for a Yankee accent."

The maids murmured agreement.

"Mrs. Whitley?"

Sally Whitley had sent a reluctant Mary Pat out to play and now looked as if she wished she could have been excused, too. "I guess we're the western branch of the new invasion," she said with a nervous laugh.

"From California, aren't you?" asked the sheriff.

"That's right. So a different accent wouldn't seem odd to Tom or me." She glanced around the room. "I don't know why Tom isn't here. Shall I go find him?"

"We talked to him up in the attic," said Dwight, "and I think he said something about measuring for cabinets he's going to build Mrs. Honeycutt."

"Then he must have told you that we've only lived here a few months ourselves. Even if we'd seen those two men, we wouldn't have realized that they didn't belong here."

"Let's see now," said Bo Poole. "I believe y'all came to Gilead when? Last September?"

"That's right. Tom's enrolled at State. We needed a place to live and Tom needed a part-time job, so when we heard that Gilead wanted a live-in caretaker—"

"It was listed with the Student Aid Office, didn't you say, Rob?" asked Dwight.

Rob nodded and started to elucidate, but Bo Poole broke in.

"I believe I heard someone say you're a teacher, Mrs. Whitley?"

"Yes. I'd applied at several schools, but all the positions were filled before we arrived. I was working part-time at a day-care center when Mr. Tyrrell called to ask if I'd look after Mary Pat full-time."

"She was a lifesaver!" Gordon said warmly. "At the last possible moment, Mary Pat's nursemaid categorically refused to leave Costa Verde. I could hardly believe our luck when I realized Gilead had a fully-certified kindergarten teacher in residence."

It was only after a quick lunch at his mother's and while he was driving back to Raleigh in time for the Carolina-

Duke semifinal, that Rob remembered that he hadn't clarified his answer to Dwight. A minor technicality, the lawyer decided. What difference did it make that Tom Whitley had approached him directly about the caretaker's job at Gilead rather than through the Student Aid Office?

Overhead the sun gradually faded and the Carolina blue sky dulled to gray. He wasn't really superstitious, Rob told himself, but he would have felt better about the upcoming game if God had left the sky blue.

"Looks as if we might have rain before dark," said Kate, glancing out the packhouse's single window.

"Maybe not."

Tom Whitley had lost a little of his initial shyness with her, but Kate was learning that the Californian was almost as sparing with words as Lacy. In the hour that they had spent measuring and planning, he hadn't offered a single personal comment. By this time, Kate would normally have the basic life history of any other workman.

Jake used to tease her about it and occasionally, when he was feeling frugal and the repairman or painter was charging fifteen or twenty dollars an hour, he would banish her to the other end of the apartment and plead with her not to come offering the man a pot of coffee and a willing ear.

"It cost us seventeen-fifty for you to hear about his wife's troubles with their daughter-in-law," he would grumble. "Couldn't you just go watch a soap opera?"

But cheerful comments and tactful questions did little to loosen Tom Whitley's tongue. "You'd think he was paying me instead of the other way around," thought Kate.

Whitley added a final notation to the long list of materials and supplies needed to convert the dark packhouse into a well-lit studio.

"I'll stop by the building supply place in Raleigh first thing Monday morning," he told Kate.

Their eyes touched briefly, then he ducked away.

"I can carry enough on my pickup to get started with till they deliver the rest."

It was his longest speech that afternoon.

In the nursery wing at Gilead, Sally Whitley paused and cocked her head in a listening attitude. She no longer heard Mary Pat's piping treble from the next room where the child had been talking to herself.

Sally rose and crossed the colorful floral carpet and peeped into the playroom. All was still and quiet.

"Mary Pat?"

She hesitated indecisively in the doorway. Technically, Mary Pat was no longer a baby and she didn't like for Sally to hover around every single minute; but if anything happened to Mary Pat, Sally thought nervously, Mr. Tyrrell would blame her.

Fortunately, before she had to decide whether or not to go hunting for her charge, she saw Mary Pat curled up on the cushioned window seat. In the last month, Mary Pat had begun to insist she was too big to take naps. As a result, she often fell asleep in odd places three or four times a week.

Relieved, Sally tucked a light blanket around the wiry little body and went back to work. For the next hour at least, she would know exactly where Mary Pat was.

She threaded clean laces into a pair of small shoes and added sneakers to the shopping list of spring clothes she was compiling. Mary Pat continued to outgrow things before she wore them out and the current sneakers were getting too tight.

Mr. Tyrrell had told her to use her own judgment, but it was probably a waste of time to pack up even these few things, thought Sally, fitting the lid on a storage box full of heavy knitted items. She knew money was no consideration, yet these were so pretty: imported, hand-worked sweaters of cashmere and mohair. Expensive, too. But knits did stretch some and unless Mary Pat grew like a weed this summer . . . at any rate, the caps and mittens would certainly go another season and she could wait until next fall to determine if the sweaters would still fit.

Assuming they were still here. Mr. Tyrrell might decide she wasn't all that good with Mary Pat, or Tom might lose control with the wrong person and—*No!*

Her thin face tightened and she pushed away that dark memory. It was only because Tom was under so much pressure at the time—that army lieutenant, the forced changeover to civilian life—even a well man would explode. And he hadn't hurt her. Not really. He'd almost gone off his head with remorse afterward and ever since, he'd been so gentle.

There was nothing to worry about, she told herself. Life here was slower paced. No pressures; only the classes at State, a few hours of physical work here on the grounds or the odd jobs like remodeling Mrs. Honeycutt's packhouse. Those army doctors were all wrong about Tom. He was just fine.

Mary Pat slept without stirring, so Sally carried the carton of winter clothes up to the attic. As she recalled, there was a trunk of summer things there from Mexico. She really ought to bring it down and see if any of them would still fit Mary Pat before they went shopping.

It was almost too warm up under the eaves of the roof. Sally slid the carton in beside Mary Pat's trunk and lifted the lid. Inside were several little sundresses and a stack of bright cotton shorts and shirts.

As long as she was up here, Sally decided, she might as well bring down the few warm weather things she and Tom had brought from California. The new matched bags stood in a neat group off to one side; but in the attic's dim light, it took her a moment to locate Tom's battered old suitcase behind an unused bedstead.

Tom had wanted to throw the bag away when they came East, but everything wouldn't fit into the new luggage her roommates had given them as a wedding present; so she'd stuffed their cutoffs, tank tops, bathing suits, and flip-flops into the case and here it had sat since last fall.

Downstairs, she stopped by the nursery to deposit Mary Pat's things and to switch on the intercom, then lugged the old bag down the back stairs to their quarters where she slung it onto the bed and clicked open the latches.

Her faded green bikini was on top. As she lifted it up, Sally felt a few grains of California beach sand sift out of the bra onto her fingers, and, for the first time, she was awash with homesickness for curling waves and salty air. Life had been so simple then, she thought wistfully: on her own, sharing an apartment with three other girls from the college, long golden evenings at the beach after a day in classes, meeting Tom there at sunset one day, and falling instantly in love with his shy gentle nature.

Remembering, her hazel eyes grew dreamy as she unpacked, then sharpened into puzzled awareness when her hands touched an unfamiliar object buried at the bottom of the suitcase. It was a small wooden box with a curved lid, about the size and shape of a loaf of bread.

She had never seen it before, but she knew without even lifting the lid that it was James Tyrrell's missing chest, and the dark fears she had been trying to push away clutched at her heart.

Tucker Sauls tore open the cellophane strip on a fresh pack of menthol cigarettes and struck a match. The smell of sulphur and tobacco made Lacy decide he was ready for another cigarette, too. He patted the large bib pocket of his overalls for his own crumpled pack. He didn't blame Tucker for switching over after that patch of pneumonia winter before last; but privately, Lacy was proud of the fact that he still smoked a man's cigarette, straight and unfiltered.

"So when you want to let's start?" asked Sauls. He leaned against the back of his logging truck, his weather-stained felt hat pushed back on his head.

Lacy squinted through the smoke. "Next week maybe. Let her get used to us coming and going first."

"What if she notices?"

Lacy snorted contemptuously. "Ain't no New York City gal gonna notice the difference between a pine tree and a peanut plant and even if she did, I got a right. Jake might of give her the farm, but he sure as hell didn't mean it for no bastard young'un," he said angrily.

Chapter Fourteen

Two weeks can make an enormous difference, especially in March, thought Kate as she walked out with Gordon and Mary Pat.

Pears, crab apples, cherries, and flowering Judas were in full bloom now. The plums had already faded and tiny fruits had begun to swell. Apple blossoms were swelling, too, and dogwoods uncurling until they were almost as wide across as a man's thumbnail, each greenish yellow petal tipped with a brownish pink "bloodstain" to symbolize the Easter legends.

Quince, spirea, forsythia, and flowering almonds were at their peak and azalea buds were showing a bit of color. Hyacinths, daffodils, and pansies crowded each other in lavish borders. Soon the irises would follow.

Confederate violets had been thick drifts of gray-blue in the orchard where Kate met Gordon and Mary Pat, and the breath-of-spring by the packhouse was covered with fresh green leaves, its scraggly twigs transformed into gracefulness. Lacy's vegetable garden had neat rows of peas, onions, and mustard, and tiny potatoes were already forming among the roots of rank green plants.

Everything seemed fecund with new life. Bluebirds were squabbling over the nesting boxes Lacy had erected around the farm, mockingbirds staked their territories with long melodic bursts of song, and Jake's lovesick pointers had deserted the farm to hang around Willy Stewart's dogpen where two of his bitches were in heat. Kate had even been kept awake last night by the yowl of mating cats.

She didn't mind. In fact, she welcomed every chirp and yowl. It was part of the natural cycle of life and she felt more and more in harmony with the farm as her own body swelled.

Two weeks had made a difference there, too. No longer could loose shirts and sweaters conceal the definite bulge of her abdomen. Now she wore proper maternity tops and slacks with stretchy stomach panels.

For Kate and Gordon, walking was therapeutic, a painless way to get the exercise their respective doctors recommended, even though Gordon was already more physically active in his newfound life as Gilead's squire.

Often when Kate walked over to meet him, she found him out on a tractor, overseeing the ditching and draining of a low field, or in conference with the farmer who currently leased the acreage allotments, about contour plowing to control erosion. He had ordered new fruit trees to rejuvenate Gilead's diseased orchard and planned to convert an idle piece of land into a modest vineyard.

"All the Tyrrells are farmers at heart," he told Kate. "I really used to envy my cousins. Not their money, but the land. They just took it for granted, while James and I felt like we'd been kicked out of Eden. If my grandfather hadn't been a younger son, I'd probably be working the family land up in Virginia right now."

Remembering the flitting, adventure-seeking life Gordon and Elaine had led, Kate was somewhat doubtful.

On the other hand, Elaine had grown up when Gilead was a rundown tobacco farm. As a child, she had risen early and gone to bed late during those hot sweaty summer days, her hands gummed with tobacco tar and her muscles aching from carrying heavy sticks of green leaves from the racks to the barns. Elaine had harbored no sentimental feelings about farming and had left as soon as Philip Carmichael's money made it possible. Kate thought Gordon might not be quite so romantic about working family land if he'd actually had to do it. Directing the labor of hired help wasn't quite the same thing.

Still, it was a harmless delusion and did not stop Kate from looking forward to their walks. Gordon was intelligent and informed and a welcome alternative to Lacy's sour company. Kate valued Miss Emily and Bessie's sturdy common sense and warm friendliness, and she supposed Rob's infrequent visits would be more enjoyable once he recovered from Carolina's poor showing in the NCAA Basketball Tournament; in the meantime, however, Gordon was someone who would talk to her about books and movies and national politics. They had fallen into the habit of meeting after lunch for a long ramble around both farms every two or three days, weather permitting; and they were usually accompanied by Mary Pat and Aunt Susie, who trailed along behind, absorbed in their own interests while the two adults talked.

The walks and the conversation with someone as content as Gordon helped calm Kate's own mercurial shifts of emotion. He seemed to have made peace with what fate had dealt him and now accepted each day's offering, while she still swung between black despair over Jake's death and deep happiness over the prospect of his child. Death and life. Mourning and exhilaration.

Both extremes were tempered by Gordon's calm steadiness, and by his immersion in the needs of the land. As he planned improvements for Gilead, he opened Kate's eyes to possible alternatives for the farm. "Tobacco's not always going to be king here," he said. "Subsidies are under attack in Congress, import restrictions will probably be loosened, and even die-hard smokers like us, Kate, are cutting back on cigarettes."

Kate had never paid much attention when Jake and Patricia talked like this; but now, carrying the baby who might someday depend on the farm for a living, she began to realize that land was not inanimate. It was a living entity with certain basic requirements that could not be safely left to renters, who often took and took with the help of chemicals, but who returned nothing organic to the soil. So as they walked, she listened when Gordon talked of cover crops, seasonal rotations, and irrigation ponds; of natural controls instead of pesticides; of windbreaks and new cash crops if tobacco stopped being profitable—asparagus, snow peas, or sunflowers. She was particularly taken with the idea of tall yellow flowers as far as the eye could see.

And she agreed that the old tobacco barns should be pulled down and the solid lumber used elsewhere.

As they passd the barns that day, Gordon gazed at the huge rusting tank that once supplied fuel to the four barns. "Did you know there's still gas in this thing?" he asked Kate.

"Is there?" She peered at the gauge and saw that it registered three-fourths full. She tapped it. The needle quivered, but remained unchanged. "Maybe it's broken."

"Maybe, but if I were you, I'd have someone come out and check it. Perhaps you could get it transferred to your house tank."

It was too nice a day to worry about economy and practicalities for long and she smiled to see Mary Pat already running across the field with Aunt Susie.

The sky above was bright blue with the puffy clouds of changeable spring weather. It had rained hard several times in the past week and the wind had blown briskly all day yesterday, so the fields were as smooth as a tabletop, and Kate had suggested that they look for arrowheads and pottery fragments.

Long before any Europeans arrived, Colleton

County had been inhabited by Indians, and late winter or early spring, before the crops were planted, was the best time to look for relics. Stray points could turn up anywhere, but the likeliest place to look was on the west side of a creek, and Jake had shown Kate an area in the lower field that had been a camp site for several tribes widely separated in time. The earliest and most beautifully detailed points dated back six thousand years; the latest and more crudely shaped were probably mid-1600s.

Mary Pat thought it was as much fun as an Easter egg hunt and she darted back and forth to show Kate and Gordon a chip of white quartz, a flake of apple-green flint or a palm-size scrap of broken pottery. The sandy field was so naturally rock-free that almost every stone was a possible Indian artifact.

"What's this?" asked Mary Pat, her grubby little hands clasped around a smooth stone the size and shape of an Idaho baking potato.

"Don't ask me," said Gordon. "Cousin Kate's the expert here."

Kate turned it in her hand, remembering the first time she had noticed a white quartz stone burned red around the outside.

"It's a pot stone. See the color? Like a brick?" she asked Mary Pat, echoing Jake's long ago explanation. "That means it's been in a hot fire."

"Why?"

"Well, you do know that Indians lived outdoors and didn't have metal pots and pans or electric stoves, don't you?"

Mary Pat nodded vigorously. "Wigwams and teepees."

When it came to Indian shelters, Kate was on shaky ground. She rather thought that wigwams and teepees went with people of the western plains while woodland tribes had built huts of woven twigs and bark, but she wasn't prepared to argue the point with Mary Pat. She really should get a book, she decided, and in the meantime, she'd stick to what Jake had told her.

"You see, the Indians that lived around here never

quite learned how to make clay pots that were strong enough to sit over a campfire; so if they wanted to cook a stew, they'd fill a pot with meat and vegetables and water and then they'd bring smooth stones like this one up from the creek and put them in the fire. When the stones were red-hot, the cook would drop two or three into the stew and begin heating the food. As soon as one cooled off, she'd fish it out, put it back in the fire and drop in another. Jake told me it didn't take much longer than cooking right over the fire."

"Stone soup!" exclaimed Mary Pat.

"Not exactly," said Kate, but she could tell from the look in the child's eyes that the connection had been made.

Gordon noted her rueful face as Mary Pat dashed across the furrows after another possible arrowhead. "What is it?" he smiled.

"I have a feeling that from now on, whenever Mary Pat hears that old folk tale about the clever beggar who tricked the stingy woman into making him soup, she's probably going to picture the fat hausfrau with feathered headband and plaited pigtails."

"If we had some ham, we'd have some ham and eggs, if we had some eggs," chanted Mary Pat.

That was one of the nonsense lines Lacy had taught her. Time hadn't helped much there and Kate began to doubt if Lacy would ever accept her presence. They walked around each other as warily as two cats and the kitchen was almost their only point of contact.

Kate had begun skipping breakfast again, waiting until Lacy went outside to do chores before she fixed herself a pot of tea; and Lacy avoided the kitchen at noon. Kate suspected that he snacked on soft drinks and cheese crackers up at Mrs. Fowler's store. Supper was a silent affair, prepared by Kate and eaten with the television tuned to a local news station. Lacy usually cleaned up the kitchen afterward and watched television till bedtime while Kate retired to her room immediately after supper to write letters, read, or jot design ideas in her notebook.

Without Miss Emily popping in or her walks with

Mary Pat and Gordon, Kate felt her vocal cords would have atrophied. Even shy taciturn Tom Whitley was more forthcoming than Lacy. If it weren't for the baby, she knew she would have fled back to New York.

Yet Jake had loved this farm, had drawn strength from the land, and renewed himself with frequent trips back. It was his child's birthright, Kate thought fiercely, and no mean-spirited, begrudging old coot was going to take that away.

Still, it was so contrary to what she had hoped for. She knew Lacy had always resented her, but to resent the baby, too? He was good with Mary Pat, patient and even playful at times, so it wasn't as if he disliked children on principle. And he'd adored Jake. How could he not look forward to the birth of Jake's child?

Ever since that Saturday when Sheriff Poole and Dwight Bryant had raised the possibility that Jake's death might have been murder, Lacy had been as prickly as a stinging nettle. Two weeks were a long time to sulk over being asked if he'd touched that envelope of Jake's war souvenirs, but Kate couldn't think of any other legitimate grievances.

"Might as well accept it once and for all," she thought. "He just doesn't like you. Never has, never will."

Into her memory floated one of her father's no-nonsense dicta: What can't be cured must be endured.

Well, she'd endure until July, she decided, following Gordon down the sloping hillside. After that, she or Lacy, one would have to leave the farm.

Running ahead of them, Mary Pat had reached the edge of the woods. Pleasantly tired, Kate and Gordon joined her on neighboring tree stumps. Mary Pat began to count the rings of one smooth stump that was nearly a yard in diameter. An oak? Poplar?

Gordon looked around approvingly. "Lacy and Sauls are making a good job of it," he said.

Kate had to agree. The two elderly men had culled out the diseased trees and cleaned up as they went. She had seen some logging stands that looked as if a tornado had gone through them, with limbs and broken tops wantonly left wherever the chain saw had cut them.

Here, though, Sauls had hauled out the logs as soon as each tree was felled, then he and Lacy piled up the brush and burned it—to keep the borers from spreading to other trees, as she had been reminded last week when she came upon the two putting a saw to the half-dozen walnut trees that lined the pecan grove on the south side of the farmhouse.

"Do they have beetles, too?" she had asked, surprised.

"Yes, ma'am," said Sauls, who turned off the saw to answer her.

Lacy had continued to swing his axe as if he didn't see her.

"You can see how these branches ain't got no green on 'em," said Sauls. "Borer beetles'll do that and you don't want 'em spreading to the pecans."

She certainly didn't. Black walnuts were so tedious to pick out—requiring a heavy hammer to crack the thick shells—that most years no one bothered to gather them. The unique flavor might be delicious, but pecans were also tasty and much easier to shell. So far, at least, the pecan trees looked healthy and were pushing out vigorous green tips. She had given a last look at the old bare-twigged walnuts and then had returned to the house before Lacy's continued snub made conversation with Sauls too uncomfortable.

Today as she and Gordon examined the lower stand of trees, one could barely tell that any cutting had occurred here beyond an occasional fresh stump. The woods were a little more open, that was all, and new growth would soon fill in the bare spots.

"Sauls says they're almost finished," said Kate. "There must be at least four cords of firewood up at the house by now."

"And another two over at Gilead that I bought from Lacy last week," said Gordon. "I know an open fireplace is an inefficient way to heat a room, but there's nothing like a pile of roaring logs to warm the spirit on a cold rainy night."

As Gordon soliloquized on the beauty of an open fire, Kate felt her own heat rise. How dare Lacy sell *her* wood to someone else!

"Lacy must be what? Seventy? Seventy-five?" asked Gordon. "I don't know where he finds the strength to do all this at his age."

Gordon's words restored Kate's sense of fairness. After all, why should she expect Lacy to work so hard for nothing? He'd said quite frankly that he and Tucker Sauls were going shares on the diseased wood and hadn't she told him to do whatever he wished? Would she go back on her word just because he might turn a few dollars extra?

She was instantly ashamed of her pettiness. Jake was gone and she was left with serious financial obligations, but that didn't mean she had to turn into a penny-pinching shrew. There was nothing so unpleasant as a person who counts the cost of everything, she lectured herself. If two or three cords of firewood or a few thousand board feet of planks could give Lacy a little financial profit, she wouldn't begrudge them. Besides, if she had to hire someone to come in and cull out the borer-infested trees, she probably would spend three times whatever Lacy and Tucker Sauls were going to make.

In a burst of generosity, Kate decided that she would pay Lacy's bill at Mrs. Fowler's store. That ought to set things even.

Seated on the next stump, Gordon drew idle patterns in the sand with the tip of his cane. Kate had been unaware of his scrutiny until he said, "I'm glad that worked out all right."

"Hm?"

"Whatever was bothering you. Your face is like a book," he teased. "First all serious as you remembered something that was bothering you, and now a satisfied that-settles-*that* look. Am I right?"

His lopsided smile made Kate smile, too.

"Very close," she said. "I've just decided I'm not

going to let Lacy Honeycutt change me into a self-pitying miser."

"Has he been trying to?" His cane nudged a fat black beetle into scuttling retreat.

"Probably not," Kate admitted. "But that's the way I've been reacting. He doesn't like me and even though the farm's mine now and I'm paying all the bills, he—"

"He isn't properly appreciative?"

His tone was sardonic and Kate flushed.

"That's not what I meant."

"No?"

"Of course not!" she said hotly. "I don't expect any praise or thanks. Not really. But Lacy acts as if CP&L gives away electricity and groceries appear in the pantry by osmosis; as if there's no connection between me and his daily comfort."

"A man as proud as Lacy Honeycutt? I imagine he's well aware of every flourish of your checkbook," said Gordon. "Very few men enjoy being kept."

There was a slight bitterness in his tone and Kate was suddenly reminded that it was Elaine's money—money that came from the sale of her family home or as an allowance from her sister Patricia—that had supported them and paid for their carefree lifestyle.

In many respects, Elaine had retained her Old South attitude toward marriage: a woman may be richer, stronger, brighter, but a good wife never lets her husband know she knows it. Publicly and, for all Kate knew, privately, too, Elaine had deferred to Gordon's wishes. They had lived in modest luxury, free to hunt, ski, and sail, and they had seemed truly affectionate and happy with each other; nevertheless, until Patricia's death gave him a separate allowance as Mary Pat's co-guardian (and that only for so long as he and Elaine remained married), Gordon had been landless gentry and dependent upon his wife's income.

Kate felt uncomfortably embarrassed, but Gordon seemed unaware of the direction his words had made her take. He looked out across the field and tried to explain Lacy to her.

"That poor old man probably doesn't have a loose

nickel to call his own. He was never in the army, so there's no military pension; and I doubt if he ever earned enough farm income to pay social security, so unless Jake left him something?"

"N-no," said Kate, stricken to realize for the first time the full extent of Lacy's poverty. "We just made simple wills. Everything to each other. I never gave it much thought, and Jake—" Her voice broke. "Jake didn't expect Lacy to outlive him."

Gordon reached over and patted her clenched hands. "I know, honey," he said. "I know. Elaine and I were the same."

In the past two weeks, they had hashed and re-hashed all the possible explanations for Jake's death and Covington's murder. If the sheriff's investigation had produced any real results, Dwight hadn't shared it with them; so Kate and Gordon kept circling back to the who and why in total frustration.

"One thing I haven't told you," said Gordon, his hand still covering hers.

She looked at him questioningly.

"I know you think Southerners put an inordinate stress on bloodlines and families. We probably get too much Old Testament drilling when we're Sunday school kids—Deuteronomy and Chronicles."

His voice slipped into a parody of a tent revivalist's singsong patter. "And I say unto you, Abraham begat Isaac, Isaac begat Jacob and Esau, and Jacob begat Reuben, Simeon, Levi, and God knows how many more besides Joseph and Benjamin."

Kate began to laugh in spite of herself.

"Anyhow," Gordon said, serious again. "I'm glad Jake begat, Kate. It's good to know that part of him continues."

Kate was moved by his earnestness. "Thank you, Gordon."

Once more Gordon remembered lying in the hospital with most of the grogginess cleared and his physical pain ebbing as he tried to get used to the idea of Elaine and his brother being gone forever. Then Rob Bryant's call had jolted him all over again with the news that Jake was dead, too. Coming when it did, that final death hit him worse than the others somehow.

"I'm the last of our Tyrrell branch and Mary Pat's the closest thing to a child of my own that I'll ever have, but I hope you'll let me share Jake's baby— maybe teach him some of the things Jake would have."

"I'd like that," Kate said tremulously.

She had never before realized that Gordon felt so warmly toward Jake. But then, she thought, it was here on a visit with James that Jake had introduced him to his cousin Elaine. Except for Jake, Gordon Tyrrell and Elaine Gilbert might never have met or fallen in love.

It was an emotional moment, an exchanged awareness of how much each of them had lost, but also of how much there was to live for. No more words were necessary. Gordon's hand dropped away and Kate sat quietly, grateful for his friendship.

They missed Mary Pat almost immediately.

A few minutes earlier, she had been perched halfway up a persimmon tree. Her little pile of Indian artifacts still lay at the foot of the tree, but she was nowhere to be seen.

"Mary Pat?" called Gordon.

The field cut into the woods so deeply at that point that, from where they sat, they could hear the creek rushing along its rocky bed in the dip beyond. Kate stood up on one of the taller tree stumps and saw a flash of Mary Pat's red sweater through the underbrush several hundred feet away.

"There she is. Mary Pat!"

The child kept going.

"She can't hear us over the creek."

"Oh, Lord," Gordon sighed, heaving himself to his feet. "Next we'll be fishing her out of the water."

They pushed through a tangle of vines and briars.

"Gordon, don't worry," Kate said. "The creek's only a couple of feet deep along here."

"She knows she's not supposed to go near it alone, though. It's not like her to disobey."

They reached the creek bank, but Mary Pat was not there. Kate scrambled over a half-submerged tree trunk and Gordon struggled to follow. His leg had strengthened in the last few weeks, but he was not yet up to cross-country broken field running.

"Be careful, Kate. You're going to fall and hurt yourself. Try calling her again."

Kate was still crashing through last winter's dead vines and fallen branches. She had spotted Mary Pat through this year's new growth.

"Come on up a little higher on the bank," she called back to Gordon. "There seems to be an old lane here."

The going was a bit easier and Gordon shouted Mary Pat's name at the top of his voice.

A few hundred feet upstream, the child turned and saw them and gaily ran back to join them.

Gordon began to scold her for coming to the creek alone.

"I wasn't going down to the water," Mary Pat protested.

One of her ponytail ribbons had come undone and Kate automatically retied the bow.

"Where *were* you going, sweetheart?" she asked, picking stray twigs and leaf scraps from the dark curls.

"I wanted to see what was shining and you and Uncle Gordon were talking and I'm not supposed to interrupt grown-ups," she said, looking up at Gordon with candid calculation.

"You're not turning into a prepubescent Portia, are you?" Gordon asked severely.

"What's that?"

"A smart-aleck little girl who obeys the letter of the law but not the spirit."

Mary Pat dropped her head. "No, sir," she whispered.

"You owe Cousin Kate an apology for worrying her like that," Gordon scolded.

"I'm sorry, Cousin Kate."

"That's better," he said. "Now let's go back and get your arrowheads and then—"

"But I want to see what's shining," said Mary Pat. "Please, Uncle Gordon."

She caught at his hand and tried to stop him, but Gordon had already turned back the way they came.

"We've walked far enough for one day," he said, still a little cross. "Cousin Kate and I are too tired for any wild-goose chases."

"I *am* getting a bit tired," Kate admitted. "I never noticed this old lane before, but it probably comes out near the highway just below Gilead. It might be shorter than walking back through the field. Easier, too, probably. Why don't we try it?"

"What about the arrowheads?"

"We could come back for them tomorrow," said Mary Pat. "Oh, please, Uncle Gordon. I really did see something shine when I was way up in the tree."

"Okay, okay," he capitulated. "Lead on, MacDuff!"

The lane meandered with the creek and was almost obscured by small trees and several years' accumulation of fallen leaves and pine needles.

"I'll bet this was Lacy's moonshine road," Kate said. "Moonshine?"

Mary Pat was several paces further on and Kate kept her voice low as she repeated Bessie and Miss Emily's tale about Lacy's moonshining days.

Gordon chuckled. "Jake once told me that the first time he was ever drunk, it was on white lightning. I didn't realize he was so young."

Ahead of them, Mary Pat plunged off the faint track and into a thick stand of young pines. Gordon and Kate followed.

"Oh, shoot! It's just an old car," said Mary Pat, disappointed to find that her something shiny was only sunlight reflected off chrome trim.

"Don't say shoot," Gordon corrected absently as he studied their unexpected find.

The late-model Chevrolet was dark green with a dull gray vinyl roof and it had been standing there for several days at least because wisteria vines had already looped a few tentative tendrils to the bumper and rear-view mirrors.

"No dents or smashed fenders. Why would anyone abandon a car like this?" Kate wondered.

Gordon opened the unlocked driver's door. "The keys are still in the ignition."

Kate flipped open the dash compartment. Inside were a car manual and rental papers. A quick perusal revealed that the car had been rented at the Raleigh-Durham Airport on the sixth of March to one C. Bernard.

Chapter
Fifteen

Kate was beginning to wonder if she'd ever get over this new propensity for drifting off to sleep whenever she got quiet and still. Cartoons flickering across the television screen had already lulled Mary Pat into a nap.

"I may take off my shoes," she had told Kate a half hour earlier.

Within ten minutes, she was curled into a tight little ball next to Kate on the couch.

Gordon had allowed enough time for the police to drive out from town; and, after telling Kate to ask the maid if she wanted more coffee, he had driven back to the creek bridge to direct the lawmen when they arrived.

That was over an hour ago.

Kate thought of her own bed with longing, but at least the study here at Gilead was furnished for comfortable lounging. She hooked the edge of a hassock with her toe and tugged it closer. As she settled herself

into the cushions, her drowsy thought was that if
Dwight Bryant didn't come soon, she was going to be
too punchy to talk.

She would have preferred to go back to the farm,
but the sheriff's office had requested that they wait
together at Gilead since Gilead was nearer the abandoned car site.

She stifled another yawn just as Sally Whitley came
into the room carrying a light afghan. With practiced
ease, Sally shifted Mary Pat out from under Kate's
elbow and covered the sleeping child.

"Would you like a blanket, too?" she asked.

"Don't tempt me," said Kate, struggling to her feet.

"Please don't get up. I'm sorry I disturbed you."

"You didn't disturb me. In fact, I'm glad you came.
Another five minutes and it would have taken dynamite
to blast me off that couch."

Kate patted her pockets in the unrealistic hope that
she might have broken her own rules. For the past
week, she'd quit taking cigarettes with her when she
went outdoors, another ploy to stretch the time between smokes. It had been almost four hours now.

"Did you want cigarettes?" asked Sally. She took a
leather box from a nearby table and held it open for
Kate.

"Oh yes, please," Kate said gratefully. "I've cut
down a lot, but I just can't seem to quit entirely."

"I've heard it's hard," said Sally.

"You've never smoked?"

"No."

There was an awkward moment, then, reluctantly,
Kate's politeness triumphed over her addiction. "If it
bothers you—"

"Oh, no!" the younger woman assured her. "Do go
ahead. Please. Tom smokes. And Mr. Tyrrell, of
course. It doesn't bother me. I just never have. I don't
know why. It's not because I'm a health nut or anything, although they *do* say—"

"They sure do," Kate sighed and guiltily struck a
match. She would only smoke half of it, she promised

herself, happily noting that the cigarette was one of the extra-long brands.

Mary Pat stirred in her sleep.

Sally looked down at the small figure indulgently. "She tells me she's too big to take naps anymore, but she almost always falls asleep after her walks with you and Mr. Tyrrell."

"They certainly do know their own minds at that age, don't they?"

Sally Whitley agreed that they did.

The conversation stalled again.

"Tom's done wonders with the packhouse," Kate said heartily. "He's zipped right through the new shelves and cabinets; even the new plumbing's finished."

"Yes, he said it was going faster than he expected."

"Was he always so handy with tools?"

"I'm not sure. I think so."

At Kate's puzzled look, Sally added shyly, "We've only known each other about a year. In fact, we met last July, right after I graduated, and got married in August."

"He *is* a fast worker," Kate smiled.

Sally blushed and smoothed her fair hair away from her face with a self-conscious gesture.

Privately, Kate marveled that two such shy people had connected that quickly.

"So how are you liking the East Coast?"

"It's okay . . . different, anyhow," Sally said with such obvious tact that Kate couldn't help smiling again.

"I was never away from L.A. before. The city, you know? Living in the country, inland and away from the ocean, is a totally new experience. For me—not like Tom."

"That's right, he was in the army for several years, wasn't he? Did he get overseas? Europe or the Far East?"

"Maybe Vietnam right at the end," Sally said uncertainly. "When he first joined up, I think. He doesn't talk about it. And Fort Bragg after that. That's why he wanted to come back here to school. He liked North Carolina."

"I would have thought he was too young for Vietnam," Kate said idly.

For some reason, her words seemed to increase Sally Whitley's self-consciousness and the young woman sprang up, murmured something about laundry chores, and hurried away.

For a moment, Kate's thoughts followed in speculation, then she shrugged and left the room herself.

In the front hall, she met Bessie's niece, who asked, "Could I get you something, Miss Kate?"

"No, thanks, DeWanda. I've decided to walk back down to the creek."

"Too late, Miss Kate. I think Mr. Tyrrell just drove up."

She opened the front door as she spoke, and Kate saw Dwight's car parked beside Gordon's and both men crossing the wide veranda.

"Sorry to keep you waiting so long," the detective apologized. He carried a boxy little black case.

"Fingerprinting time," Gordon warned her dryly.

"What?"

"We need to get yours and Mr. Tyrrell's and the little girl's, too," Dwight said.

"Now just a minute," said Gordon, pausing in his tracks. "I've agreed to let you take mine, and Mrs. Honeycutt may not mind having her fingerprints on file, but I'm certainly not going to let Mary Pat's be punched into some big brother computer. Perhaps we'd better forget the whole thing."

"That won't happen, Mr. Tyrrell," Dwight said patiently. "This is just for local use. See, we'll send all the fingerprints we find on that car to the FBI. As soon as they eliminate the ones that belong to you three, they'll destroy your cards. Anyhow," he reminded Gordon, "we wouldn't have to be doing this if y'all hadn't messed with the car."

Reluctantly, Gordon led him into the dining room and Kate watched as he inked Gordon's fingers and rolled each one onto a special card. He was repeating the process with her fingers when a sleepy-eyed Mary Pat, still in stocking feet, found them there.

She was interested to learn that her fingers might have left invisible marks on the car she'd found; but she was still too recently awake to ask her usual questions, and she offered no resistance when Sally Whitley appeared and led her off to the kitchen for a glass of milk.

"This is going to help a lot, y'all finding that car," said Dwight, packing up his fingerprint kit. "From the rental papers, it looks like Bernie Covington was traveling under a simple alias—he just reversed his initials and used his real first name for a last name. He would've had to show a charge card and driver's license to rent a car and they should have records. With a little luck, we can maybe trace back where he's been and what he's been doing since he skipped bail in Florida."

"Did you ever hear from the Mexican police?" Kate asked, abruptly remembering all their unanswered questions.

"Well," Dwight said slowly, "yes, we did."

"And?" asked Gordon.

Dwight became evasive. "I probably ought to let Sheriff Poole talk to you about that."

"What's that supposed to mean?" Gordon asked sharply. "Have they found part of the boat?"

"Not exactly. We got a picture of Covington from California, where he served time, and sent it down to Costa Verde. Seems there's a pretty little señorita—leastways she sounds like she might be pretty—she remembers seeing your brother have dinner with this Covington two nights before the accident."

"Covington in Costa Verde?" asked Gordon, amazed. "With James? She's sure?"

"Police there say she knew Mr. James Tyrrell pretty good. A Margarita Somebody-or-other."

"Margarita Ruiz," Gordon nodded. "She sings at one of the clubs there. James took her out a couple of times. She *is* pretty. But James with Covington? He never mentioned it."

He sounded puzzled by his brother's reticence.

"She recognized the picture of Covington. Said she saw him again a month later. Desk clerk at one of the hotels remembers seeing him, too, but he can't remember when it was. If Covington stayed in town, he didn't register under his own name. Sort of odd, isn't it, that your brother didn't say something about running into one of his old army buddies?"

Gordon spread his hands helplessly. "Maybe he did. There's so much about that time that I can't remember. This could be one more thing that I've forgotten."

"You reckon?" Dwight asked dubiously. He moved to leave, then paused in the doorway. "Can I give you a lift down the turnpike, Kate? I need to ask Mr. Lacy how come he didn't notice that car before now."

Driving back to the farmhouse, Kate was thoughtful as Dwight negotiated the lane's sandy ruts.

"Did the Costa Verde police say anything about a younger man with Covington?"

"You mean that kid that was on patrol with them?"

"Yes."

"Nope. Not a word. According to that señorita, he had dinner with James Tyrrell alone."

Kate sighed. "It just doesn't make sense, Dwight. If Covington caused that boating accident, why was he still in Costa Verde a month later? And if he *was* in Mexico then, how could he be connected with Jake's death up here?"

"Too soon to tell," said Dwight, skirting the orchard and rolling to a stop near the kitchen porch.

"And with James and Jake both dead, why did Covington's rental car wind up on our creek bank?" she asked. "Why would he come back at all?"

The burly detective had opened his door, but he hesitated with one foot in and the other on the ground. "I can't say why, but we do know how the car got there. There's a pull-off place beside the bridge that some of the old-timers fish from once in a while. It's rough driving, but not too hard once you strike into that old track along the bank. We found snapped-off undergrowth, so we can tell the car came in from the highway and not from your woods.

"Whoever killed Covington might have met him in the packhouse after you and Mr. Lacy went to bed. After he killed Covington, he was probably left with two cars, so he stashed Covington's down there and walked back for his own. I reckon he thought that dark green color was as good as camouflage if he stuck it deep enough into some dark green trees."

Kate shivered. "That means the killer's been hanging around the farm long enough to know about that old lane beside the creek. Since last October, maybe?"

"Maybe."

"Then he could still be here—walking in and out of our houses, stealing pictures and papers." She stared at Dwight. "Camouflage and night maneuvers! It *is* someone they knew in Vietnam, isn't it?"

"Well, that's how it looks to me," said Dwight. "We think we've got a name on that kid: William Thompson."

Kate remembered the "W.T." Jake had scribbled on the back of one of the missing snapshots. "Has he been located?"

"Not yet. Nobody seems to know what happened to him or where he is now, twelve years later. In the meantime, no matter who put the car down yonder at the creek, I don't see how Mr. Lacy missed it if he's been culling over your woods."

Kate was not surprised to realize that Dwight knew everything that was going on here at the farm—not with Miss Emily and Bessie to keep him posted—but she got a demonstration of his trained powers of observation as they crossed the yard to the chicken pen where Lacy was gathering eggs.

She had walked right past Lacy's dilapidated old pickup without a second glance, but Dwight's first comment after he greeted Lacy was, "I see you got that ol' mule of yours a new set of shoes."

Kate turned and saw the truck's gleaming black

tires. Now that Dwight had remarked on them, she
could even smell the fresh new rubber.

"It were about time," Lacy said defensively. "Them
other ones was as slick as Tucker Sauls's bald head."

"Yeah, I noticed," Dwight grinned. "I was wondering how you passed your last inspection."

Lacy was disinclined to bandy words across a poul-
try yard with the younger man. Remaining just outside
the chicken house, he shifted the egg basket in his
hand and said, "What can I do for you, Dwight?"

"It's about that dead man, Mr. Lacy. Kate and Mr.
Tyrrell found his car this afternoon."

The old farmer's eyes flicked over Kate stonily,
but he listened without comment while the chickens
pecked around his feet and the rooster, a big Rhode
Island Red, ruffled his neck feathers in mild disapproval of their closeness beyond the fence wire.

"It was down on the creek bank," said Dwight.
"Somebody drove it in from the highway and left it in
a little stand of young pines."

"That right?"

Kate recognized that Lacy was getting ready to dig
in his heels and become as uncooperative as possible
and suddenly, she was too tired to put up with any
more of his irritating mannerisms.

"There's no need to make a big deal out of this,
Lacy. Everyone knows you and Tucker Sauls have
looked at every tree on the place. Nobody's spying on
you or prying into your private affairs. All Dwight
wants to know is if you were in that part of the woods
since Covington was killed so he'll know whether the
car's been there the whole time or not."

Surprisingly, Lacy climbed down off his high horse.
He didn't exactly answer Kate, but he did tell Dwight,
"We walked that stretch of creek last month. Didn't
see no borer beetles along there, so I didn't have no
occasion to go back, and if she found any car there, I
can't rightly say when it come. Not afore Washington's
Birthday, anyhow. His real birthday. 'Cause that's the
very day I was there—February 22. Mail didn't run on

Monday, but Wednesday was his real birthday and I remarked on that to Sauls when we was walking back to the truck."

Artificial holidays were a pet peeve with Lacy even though Jake used to get down more often because of them. Having never planned his life around a forty-hour work week, Lacy didn't hold with messing up the calendar just to give city folks some extra three-day weekends.

Amusement mingling with exasperation, Kate left the two men at the chicken yard and headed for the house. Baby or no baby, she decided she deserved something a little stronger than iced tea before she began supper.

Chapter Sixteen

Dwight Bryant shared Sheriff Poole's enthusiasm for the modern tools of law enforcement: the chemicals that could develop fingerprints years after they were laid down; the Identi-Kits that could build up composites into such lifelike pictures that witnesses would say, "Yeah, that's him! That's the man who robbed the Winn-Dixie last night"; the serological tests that linked victim with killer; or, most useful of all, the space-age electronic PIN terminal which occupied a tabletop in their nineteenth-century courthouse office.

Operated by the FBI, the Police Information Network connected their little force with the largest in the nation and there was nothing to touch it for tracing stolen guns, stolen cars, or persons with criminal records; but for information of a local nature, a detective asking his own questions face-to-face was still the best road to go, thought Dwight, as he buttered up the matronly manager of a rental car concession just off the main lobby of the Raleigh-Durham air terminal.

It was Tuesday morning and already the sprawling terminal was surprisingly crowded. Basketball might get local adrenaline flowing, but the universities reached wider than sports. Duke and Carolina had always attracted foreigners to their medical programs, and State's agriculture and engineering schools had international reputations. So with the growth of the Research Triangle, Asian and Middle Eastern faces and accents had long since lost their novelty, and bursts of French, Dutch, or German mingled easily with the y'alls and drawls.

Half flirting, half flattering, while flight passengers from a dozen countries came and went, Dwight learned that the rental manager's mother had been born and raised in Colleton County.

"In fact, Mama was a Matthews from the Leach Crossroads area."

The deputy was delighted to hear it. "She wouldn't have been kin to Sammy Matthews, would she?" he asked, naming a man in that neighborhood with whom he had a nodding acquaintance.

"Why, Sammy Matthews is my second cousin! You know him?"

"We've met a few times," said Dwight. "Knew his daddy better."

"Uncle Hassie?"

"Hassie Matthews," Dwight nodded. "He's buried at my church. Fine upstanding old gentleman."

"He certainly was," agreed the woman. "And Aunt Naomi, too."

Reassured that their corner of North Carolina was still a small world, she willingly checked her log sheets and called over the young clerk who had rented "Charles Bernard" a green and gray Chevrolet nearly three weeks ago.

The small, dark-haired girl had an oriental tilt to her heavily made-up eyes, yet she was just as willing to help. Unfortunately, nothing about Bernie Covington's picture or the graphic description of the black mole on his cheek rang even the smallest bell.

Yes, that was her entry for Charles Bernard on the

log sheet, so yes, she must have taken the man's charge card, looked at his driver's license, and eventually handed over the keys to the Chevrolet; but that was also their busiest time of the day and whether he'd been alone or traveling with a dozen people was impossible to know.

The big deputy thanked them for their time and trouble and was turning to go when a second thought occurred to him. "I don't reckon you keep records as far back as six months, do you?"

"I reckon we sure do," said the manager. "What date you looking for?"

They went into her tidy office behind the rental desk and Dwight asked her to work back from that October Sunday when Jake Honeycutt was killed.

According to the log sheets, a C. Bernard had rented a Datsun on the second Friday in October and had turned it back in the following Sunday night.

It was like scoring a thirty-foot basket at the buzzer, Dwight thought happily. No pom-pom girls, no chanting crowds, only the matronly rental agent to cheer him on; yet, as he headed toward the main lobby to find out how good the airline records were, he felt as if he were taking the ball downcourt for a slam dunk.

Kate led Rob Bryant to the middle of the remodeled packhouse and gestured with proprietary pleasure. "Voilà!"

The redheaded lawyer had stopped by on his way to an afternoon meeting in Fayetteville, and he'd found Kate superintending the finishing details on her new studio.

She wore jeans and an oversized green maternity sweater that changed her eyes to green, too. Her shoulder-length brown hair was looped back from her face with a ribbon and her skin was lightly tanned from her daily walks. Despite Lacy's continued disapproval, Covington's murder, and the mystery surrounding Jake's death, these weeks in the country had helped

Kate. She was still too thin, but her eyes were clear and her hands were steady. Rob knew that Bessie and his mother were partly responsible. Ever since the two women had decided that "Kate could use some fattening up," a steady supply of nourishing casseroles and tempting goodies had issued from both kitchens.

Now the object of their concern pirouetted in a model's turn and pointed to the large expanse of glass that replaced the north wall. "Isn't it beautiful, Rob?"

Her brown hair swung golden in the clear light and her lovely face tilted toward his with such radiance that there was a sudden catch in his emotions.

Beautiful indeed, he thought; but she was talking about the room of course, so he dutifully examined the tilt-top drawing table, the swivel stool, and the new shelves and counters that would soon be stocked with the tools of her trade. There was a movement in one of the deep cupboards and Rob stooped for a closer look.

"Boo!" said Mary Pat from her niche, and dissolved into giggles as he jumped back in mock fright.

A couple of gray kittens skittered along the bare shelf; the other two crouched in her lap.

A wide ledge had been built under the large window between two sets of counters and Bessie Stewart gave Rob a distracted smile as she measured and jotted her figures on a scrap of paper.

"Bessie thinks I need a place to nap, so she's going to make cushions for the window seat," Kate explained.

"It'll do for the baby, too," said Bessie, ever practical. "Push you a couple of chair backs up real close so he can't roll out—be just like a playpen."

"Tom says I can start moving in this afternoon," Kate said. "It's all finished except for wiring the fluorescent fixtures to the fuse box, right, Tom?"

"And painting the outside," said Whitley, ducking his head self-consciously as he knelt on the floor and continued to tack weather stripping around the underedge of the solid new trapdoor he'd built to replace the broken one.

The smell of new wood and fresh paint almost overcame the odor of damp tobacco-permeated earth that rose through the opening.

Originally, Kate had considered flooring over the entire opening, but matching the wide planks would have been difficult and besides, a trapdoor might be useful if she ever wanted to convert the pit into proper storage space.

"You've really done a professional job here, Tom," Rob said, looking down into the pit at the newly-mended steps.

The outer door to the pit was open down below and sunlight spilled inside, lighting up the gloomy interior. A bundle of old tobacco sticks had been neatly repiled beside some scraps of lumber and Formica left over from the remodeling. Several dusty jugs of cider were grouped on the ground near the back and Aunt Susie, Lacy's old beagle hound, was nosing among the jugs and jumping back with soft excited little yelps.

"What's she found?" asked Rob.

"One of the kittens?" hazarded Tom Whitley.

"All my kitties are here," said Mary Pat, pushing between the two men for a better view.

Aunt Susie looked at the humans clustered on the stairs and gave a sharper bark.

"Another mouse," Kate said with a resigned air. "We've caught three already."

Rob armed himself with one of the four-foot tobacco sticks and followed Aunt Susie's lead. He poked behind the cider jug that interested her most, then abruptly jerked the stick back even faster than the dog's retreat.

"Snake!" he said hoarsely.

"*Snake?*" squealed Kate and hastily fled back up the steps, scooping Mary Pat up in her arms as she went.

"Where? Where?" said Mary Pat, struggling to see, but Kate was too frightened to let her down.

All her life, she'd had an instinctive, unreasoning fear of snakes, and the thought of this one's nearness made her tremble and clutch Mary Pat even tighter.

"All the banging I've done lately probably woke him out of hibernation early," said Whitley, peering over

Rob's shoulder at the sluggish creature that lay in loose black loops around the cider jugs. "Anybody have a shotgun handy?"

"What you talking shotgun for?" asked Bessie, who'd come up behind them.

"You're right, Bessie," Rob said. "No point in smashing Lacy's cider. As slow as he's moving, I could probably fish him out with a hoe and then chop his head off."

Bessie gave a disgusted snort. "Where your eyes at, boy? You been living in Raleigh so long you don't know a blacksnake from a cottonmouth no more?"

She looked back up to Kate, who stood well away from the trapdoor opening, still holding Mary Pat. "You don't need to be afraid of him, honey," she said reassuringly. "It's just an old blacksnake. He'll keep the mice and rats down for you."

"Oh, no, please, Bessie!" Kate implored. "Let Rob kill it. I couldn't bear to know it's crawling around down there. *Please!*"

There was such panic in her voice that Bessie said, "Well, if you're sure you don't want him—"

To Kate's horrified disbelief, Bessie reached down among the jugs, grasped the snake firmly behind the head and lifted its muscular three-foot length with gentle confidence.

In her blue print dress and white apron, with sunlight turning her gray hair into spun silver, Bessie turned to them as if it were the most natural thing in the world to have a snake coiled around her arms. "Any tow bags still up there, Kate? He's too heavy for me to carry like this."

Kate looked around wildly for a substitute. "We burned all the trash. Would a paper bag do?"

"Ah," came Gordon's voice from outside the pit door. "I *thought* I heard voices around here."

He started to enter just as Bessie turned. The snake writhed in her arms.

"Oh my God!" Gordon exclaimed and nearly stumbled over backward in his haste to get out of her way.

Bessie clicked her tongue impatiently. "You folks

beat all I ever seen! He's scareder of y'all than y'all are of him."

The snake was wide-awake now and he did not look scared to Kate. He looked mad enough to bite and she was glad when Bessie gathered her big white apron up into a makeshift sack and dumped the sinuous creature safely inside.

"Lots of girls don't like no kind of snake and maybe they's only poisonous ones out in California," Bessie said, giving Tom Whitley the benefit of doubt. "But *you*, Robbie Bryant! You used to catch snakes and lizards, too, when you was little and chase those Gilbert girls all over creation."

"Just garter snakes, Bessie," Rob protested. "I never picked up any rat snakes that big."

She didn't bother to argue with him. "I'll just step across the road and put him in our barn, Kate—old Nebuchadnezzar went and got hisself 'lectrocuted in the transformer last fall. Time I thought about fixing Willy his dinner, anyhow."

There was a sheepish silence as Bessie's sturdy little figure struck off on the footpath that led directly through the wooded triangle to the Stewart house.

"I suppose snakes do play some sort of role in the ecological chain," Kate said doubtfully.

"I've heard they eat a lot of rodents," said Tom Whitley.

"It was just seeing one so unexpectedly like that," said Gordon with an involuntary shudder.

"Don't feel bad," Rob said kindly. "You couldn't pay me enough money to pick up any kind of snake anymore."

"Me neither!" said Mary Pat from her perch atop Gordon's shoulder.

Chapter
Seventeen

Over a simple lunch of soup and grilled cheese, Sally Whitley listened happily to Tom's description of the snake discovery. He was in such high spirits that she wished to prolong the mood.

"Was Mr. Tyrrell scared, too?"

"Scared? Oh, Sally, you should have seen him trying to get out of the pit once he saw that thing! His feet were still coming in, but his head wanted out. That fancy walking stick got caught in the door and I thought he'd either break it or break his leg before he got everything moving in the right direction!"

Sally giggled at the picture Tom drew.

It was not a malicious giggle. Gordon Tyrrell had been courteous and fair in his dealings with them. He did not make unreasonable demands on their time nor burden them with nit-picking duties, but he was still an employer. *Their* employer. A bit too distant, a little too dignified. It was always amusing to see authority's dignity ruffled.

"Mary Pat said she wanted to follow Bessie Stewart home and watch where she put the snake, but Mr. Tyrrell wouldn't let her," said Sally.

Tom had given Tyrrell and Mary Pat a lift back to Gilead in his pickup, and he had heard the warning Tyrrell gave his young niece about touching strange snakes, no matter what Bessie's example.

"He's right, too," said Tom. "This state has almost every kind of poisonous snake going: copperheads, moccasins, rattlers—when I was at Fort Bragg, one of the guys even found a coral snake. Our sergeant told us that a copperhead would make you good and sick if you didn't get help right away, but a coral snake could make you good and dead."

Sally shivered lightly even though she'd never seen a snake in the wild.

"Want more soup?"

She had brought a panful from the main kitchen to keep hot on the stove in their efficiency kitchen. If pressed for time, they occasionally ate lunch in the staff room; however, they were still so newly-married that both preferred to have their meals alone, together, and Mrs. Faircloth often made something special for "the honeymooners," as she called them.

Tom glanced at his watch and shook his head. "No time. Class starts in forty-five minutes, so I'd better hit the road. I may be a little late this afternoon. I told Mrs. Honeycutt I'd pick up a few gallons of exterior paint. She wants me to match that faded red."

"Think you can?"

"No problem." He took a crumpled card smeared with rosy color from his pocket. "We experimented with some of her inks till we got a good match. I think a bright red would be better, but she knows what she wants—makes up her mind and sticks to it," he said admiringly.

He picked up his books, kissed her, and was off, leaving Sally feeling vaguely diminished. She knew all too well that she dithered, that her firmest decisions were almost always undone by second thoughts.

She put their dishes in the tiny sink and went to see if Mary Pat had finished lunch.

In the dining room, she found the little girl toying with a cluster of grapes she obviously didn't want. Her eyelids looked heavy and she gave a big yawn as Sally appeared.

"I believe somebody could use a nap," Gordon Tyrrell smiled.

"Aren't we going to walk with Cousin Kate?" The question was half protest.

"Not today, honey. She's busy and I have letters to write. You go along with Sally now and rest a little while, all right?"

"Yes, sir."

She slipped down from the silk brocade chair and followed Sally upstairs.

This was a time Sally enjoyed. She washed the sticky face and hands, untied the shoelaces, and together they chose a storybook. Mary Pat was an affectionate child and she climbed onto Sally's lap to hear Dr. Seuss's gentle nonsense. *Horton Hatches the Egg* was her current favorite; but Sally looked forward to the day when Mary Pat would be old enough for *Watership Down* or the Tolkien books.

If they were still here. She had grown so fond of Mary Pat that the thought of ever leaving was a sad one.

Sally liked to read aloud; and under the spell of the printed page, her normally light voice became firm and dramatic.

"And it should be, it *should* be, it SHOULD be like that! Because Horton was faithful! He sat and he sat! He meant what he said and he said what he meant. And they sent him home happy, one hundred percent!"

"One hundred percent," Mary Pat echoed with a great sigh of satisfaction that everything had ended happily once again despite the Mayzie-bird threat.

Impulsively, she turned her lips to Sally's cheek and gave her a quick kiss. Sally hugged her back and they rocked in comfortable silence for a few minutes. "Sing about Puff," she murmured sleepily.

Sally's voice was thin but true and she turned "Puff the Magic Dragon" into a lullaby. Mary Pat snuggled deeper in her arms and soon fell asleep.

The chair rocked slowly and Sally began to feel somewhat drowsy herself, but there was something she needed to do; so she carried Mary Pat over to the bed, switched on the intercom, and tiptoed out.

The stairway just beyond Mary Pat's door led directly down to a vestibule that separated the kitchen area from the Whitleys' quarters. Through the closed swinging doors, Sally could hear the television in the staff room.

This was always a quiet period of the day. After lunch was served and the kitchen put in order, Mrs. Faircloth and the maids usually watched soap operas for an hour or so while they rested.

For the past two weeks, Sally had dithered over the cedar chest that she'd found in the suitcase. Alone, she had taken out each item and carefully examined it: the torn map, the pictures, the discharge papers, a crumpled brass bullet shell, a carved ivory bead, and half a dozen other bits and pieces of war souvenirs.

She had sneaked an atlas from the study, but its map of Vietnam was too small to correlate to the damaged terrain map which had neither latitude nor longitude markings.

The pictures were only a little better. There were names on the backs, so she could pick out which was the dead man and even though Mr. Tyrrell was clean-shaven and his brother had worn a mustache, she could see a resemblance about the eyes and the tilt of his head, enough to identify which was James Tyrrell. The other man, taller and really good-looking, must be Mrs. Honeycutt's husband.

It gave Sally goose pimples to realize that those pictures had been taken only twelve or thirteen years ago and now all of them were dead. All except the slender boyish figure that stood off to one side and squinted in the sunlight as if he were too shy to push in with the other men.

They had called him Kid and he looked so incredibly young that she couldn't understand how the army could have let him enlist. Of the four, he would have changed the most over the years. The bones would have tightened, the face firmed into manhood. He probably looked nothing like this picture now.

Was that why she couldn't decide what to do? Was it because she honestly didn't think these pictures would help the sheriff locate the boy, or because she'd have to tell how and where she had found the chest? She couldn't do that without first asking Tom why he had taken it from James Tyrrell's trunk and hidden it in their dilapidated old suitcase.

And she couldn't bring herself to ask him.

For the past week, the suitcase had been stuffed under their bed, unnoticed by Tom and untouched by her, while she tried to make up her mind about it.

Sometimes, she thought, not deciding could be a decision.

Now, while the house was quiet and Mary Pat's curious eyes were closed in sleep, she would take the suitcase back up to the attic and put it where she had found it. Next week, she could casually tell Tom it would soon be time for summer shorts and swimsuits. Together, they would bring the suitcase down and maybe then he would confide in her—tell her what it was about Vietnam that still festered inside him.

When she turned the knob, a sudden draft caught the door as cool air whistled through the rooms. Her first thought was that Tom had rushed back for a forgotten book or paper and hadn't closed the outer door properly.

Her second thought was that he'd been awfully messy about trying to find whatever he'd misplaced.

Then, with a shock much colder than the mild spring air swirling around her, she realized that someone else, not Tom, had pulled out all their drawers, tumbled his books on the floor, and plundered the closets.

Mom's earrings!

Her jewelry was department store quality except for
her wedding band and a pair of ruby and pearl earrings
which was all she had left of her mother.

Her father wasn't wealthy, but he liked to give jewelry and the earrings had been a special gift to mark
Sally's birth. After her mother died two years ago, he
had promptly remarried a woman who took possession
of everything except those earrings. Her father insisted
that Sally should have them even though his new wife
sulked for a week.

With sinking heart, Sally rushed into the bedroom
and found an even greater mess. Her jewelry box was
upside down on her dresser and, yes, the earrings were
gone.

A wave of nausea swept over her. For a moment,
she felt as if she would either faint or throw up; then
the mists cleared and she saw that the thief had pulled
the old suitcase from its hiding place under the bed.

It took only another moment to confirm that the
little cedar chest was missing, too.

A dozen possibilities raced through her mind and
were immediately blotted out by the knowledge that
she couldn't raise an alarm until that suitcase was safely
back in the attic. No one must know about it. Not even
Tom.

Especially not Tom.

She hastily repacked their summer things and carried the suitcase out to the vestibule. Except for the
television, there was no sound or movement beyond
the swinging doors.

She raced up the stairs on silent feet, past Mary
Pat's door, and quietly eased open the door to the attic
steps.

In less than two minutes, she was back in her own
rooms again, out of breath, yet literally breathing easier
because no one had seen her.

James Tyrrell's chest had been a worrisome problem
and she did not regret that it was out of her hands
now, but as she pushed through the swinging doors to
announce the theft, the knowledge that her mother's

earrings were probably gone forever made her throat tight with unshed tears.

Dwight Bryant was driving back to Dobbs, was practically there in fact, when the car radio crackled with his own call signal. By the time he got to Gilead, his colleagues had almost finished processing the Whitley's quarters for fingerprints and clues; and Gordon Tyrrell was trying to comfort Sally.

"I'll put ads in all the local papers," he promised. "Five hundred dollars reward and no questions asked."

"Oh, no," she said. "I couldn't let you do that. They weren't worth that much. Not in in m-money anyhow."

Her voice broke again and Gordon looked helpless.

The maid DeWanda put her arm around Sally and hugged her like a baby and Mary Pat's own lips quivered sympathetically as she patted Sally's hand and said, "Don't cry, Sally. We'll all look and we'll find your earrings, won't we, Uncle Gordon?"

"I don't know, honey. I hope so."

He turned to the detectives. "This has got to stop, Bryant! Enough's enough. Murder—theft—it's about time you caught the fellow."

"What do you suggest?" Dwight asked courteously.

"How should I know? Bloodhounds? Twenty-four-hour surveillance of the neighborhood? You're the professional. What does it take to make us safe in our houses again?" There was as much frustration as anger in his voice. "I don't blame you personally, but don't you see? It has to stop!"

Dwight understood how violated people felt after a burglary.

"We can put a man on patrol," he said, "but unfortunately, the day of not locking your doors is gone, Mr. Tyrrell. There's no sign that this one was forced. Whoever did it, he just opened the door and walked in."

Sally Whitley looked even more miserable. "It never occurred to me," she said. "We lock up at night, of course, but during the daytime—" She glanced at her employer guiltily.

"No one blames you, Sally," Gordon assured her. "Maybe it was just a tramp, some guy who thought he was knocking at the kitchen door to ask for a handout and then, when you didn't answer, helped himself to whatever he could find."

He'd been very lucky, Dwight decided after hearing all their stories—the cook and maids in after-lunch siesta in front of the television, Tom Whitley off to school, Sally upstairs with Mary Pat, Gordon Tyrrell also upstairs writing letters in his room.

Or was it luck?

According to Sally Whitley, this was Tuesday's typical routine unless Mr. Tyrrell and Mary Pat walked with Kate Honeycutt. A careful watcher might be able to deduce the pattern.

The same careful watcher who had known about the creek path? Who had killed Covington, walked unseen through the Honeycutt farmhouse, plundered Gilead's attic?

"You're sure he didn't take anything besides your earrings?" Dwight asked again.

"N-no, nothing," Sally said tearfully.

Chapter
Eighteen

Mary Pat Carmichael sat cross-legged on the floor by her toy box feeling slightly muddled. Everything kept changing but she had thought she understood the game the grown-ups were playing with the little wooden box: somebody was supposed to hide it and then everybody else try to find it.

First it was in Uncle James's trunk and when Sally found it and hid it, Uncle Gordon called people in to help look. Then she found it in that old suitcase under Sally's bed; only when Sally called everybody in to look, she didn't tell them about the little box. Just her earrings. And Sally had cried, so maybe earrings weren't part of the game, just the box.

Mary Pat knew that prying was rude, and she would never open someone else's drawers or closets uninvited; nor did she ever enter without permission Gordon Tyrrell's rooms or the servants' locker room where they changed clothes and left their pocketbooks. There were rules against that and Mary Pat obeyed specific rules.

But Sally had given her free run of their quarters when she and Tom were there and no one had said she mustn't enter alone; so there was no feeling of breaking any rules, only a slight sense of mischief that made Mary Pat click on the intercom in the playroom a few days ago and then slip down the stairs to Sally's bedroom. Through the intercom panel over the double bed, she could listen as Sally vacuumed and sang to herself directly overhead.

Mary Pat had done this before; but that day, as she reached for the intercom button, her hand jiggled a pencil on the shelf that formed the headboard and it rolled off the back. She lifted the edge of the coverlet and started to crawl under the bed, to find an old suitcase blocking her way.

She pulled it out, retrieved the pencil, and started to push the bag back under when curiosity overcame her. There was a brief struggle with her conscience; but somehow, a shabby, beat-up suitcase didn't seem in the same category as drawers and cupboards. And after she opened it, she was thrilled to discover the little wooden box that all the adults had hunted for the week before.

Giggling to herself, she had replaced the suitcase and carried the little box off to a new hiding place, thinking how much fun it would be when Sally discovered it was gone. Because that was part of the game. You weren't supposed to even hint that you were the one who knew where it was.

Only, Sally wasn't playing the way Uncle Gordon did. Unless—?

Another possibility suddenly popped into Mary Pat's mind: Maybe Sally didn't know. Maybe it was *Tom* who had hidden the little box under their bed. And some bad person really did sneak in and steal Sally's pretty earrings.

Poor Sally, she thought.

Mary Pat truly regretted Sally Whitley's sadness, but she was only four and a half years old and she could not resist hugging to herself her secret knowledge of James Tyrrell's perambulating cedar chest.

That first hiding place was no good, she decided happily. She knew a much better one.

News of the latest theft spread quickly from DeWanda to Bessie to Kate.

Kate had hauled a carload of cartons from the front parlor down to the packhouse and she stopped unpacking when Bessie came back in mid-afternoon with a jug of iced tea, some freshly-baked cookies, and an account of Sally Whitley's loss.

"That poor child!" said Bessie. "Now she's got nothing left of her mama's. It's so sad."

Kate went blank for a moment, trying to remember if she had a single keepsake from either of her own parents. She couldn't think of anything. Her mother had sold all her Carmichael heirlooms long before Kate's birth. Both parents were scholars and conscientious nonmaterialists who lived Spartan lives, were indifferent to most nonintellectual activities, and supported a dozen or more worthy causes around the globe. They were slightly startled when Kate came along in their late thirties; and, although they tended her well and kindly, they never quite overcame their conviction that childrearing was some sort of intellectual exercise in logic and efficiency.

Kate was thirteen before she saw the humor of the whole situation and stopped feeling sorry for herself. In their own way, she knew they felt affection for her. They would not come East for the birth of their grandchild, but eventually there would arrive in her mailbox a notification from some animal-of-the-month club that an endangered dikdik or howler monkey had been adopted in the baby's name.

Kate abruptly realized that Bessie was staring at her curiously, so she nodded, "Yes, it *is* sad. And scary, too, if it's the same person that killed that man and stole Jake's war things. I wonder if Dwight thinks it was?"

"DeWanda said he didn't rightly say. Mr. Gordon,

he thought it was a tramp." The shrug of her shoulder dismissed Gordon Tyrrell's theory. "Have some more cookies, honey. Oatmeal's real good for you."

Smiling, Kate took another, moist with raisins and still warm from Bessie's oven. The domestic aroma of oatmeal and molasses made her feel cossetted.

"I'd tell you they tasted just like my mother used to make, only my mother never baked a thing in her life," Kate said, and gave the older woman a hug as she went back to unpacking her drawing supplies.

Bessie was shocked, and her mouth pursed disapprovingly while she measured the window seat for cushions. She knew times had changed, that working mothers couldn't bake as often as they might wish, that store-bought cakes and cookies often had to fill in; but what kind of mother never baked at all?

As she carefully wrote down the final figures, she heard a car pull up outside. Kate had heard, too, and went over to a new window beside the door.

"Why, here's Dwight now," she said and opened the door.

The detective looked at the half-eaten cookie in her hand. "That's not one of Bessie's, is it?"

Kate laughed at the hopeful look on his face and called back over her shoulder, "Here I thought he'd come to tell us about the latest crime and all he wants is one of your cookies, Bessie."

"He always could sniff 'em out," said Bessie. "Beatingest thing I ever saw."

But her dark face beamed as she lifted the napkin from the heaped plate and invited him to help himself.

Dwight did not stand on ceremony. He took three cookies in rapid succession and washed them down with a paper cup of iced tea. "I could smell 'em from the top of the turnpike, Bessie," he grinned and promptly ate two more.

"Now what's all this we hear 'bout somebody breaking in at Gilead again?" Bessie asked guilelessly, refilling Dwight's cup from the tea jug.

"You gonna pretend like DeWanda didn't give you a blow-by-blow account?" he teased.

"She might of hit the high spots," Bessie admitted, "but Kate didn't hear her."

Whether it was the cookies that loosened his tongue or for reasons of his own, Dwight described the burglary in greater detail than DeWanda had been able to. Kate stretched her long legs out on the window ledge and Bessie perched on the high stool to listen, while Dwight found himself a seat on a countertop and told how the outer doorknob to the Whitley rooms had been wiped clean and how no unexpected fingerprints had been found anywhere else.

"Was it the same man as before?" Kate asked.

"Hard to say. Sure doesn't sound like Mrs. Whitley's earrings have anything to do with the rest of what's happened."

"It's been almost three weeks," Kate said bleakly. "We're never going to know, are we?"

She was suddenly seized by another of those irrational mood swings as she thought of Jake, killed before her pregnancy was confirmed. He had wanted a child as much as she and to die without knowing—it was so damnably unfair!

"Whoever it was, he's done what he came to do, got what he wanted, and now he's gone. Jake was murdered and we'll never know who did it or even why."

Her head fell and her hair swirled around her thin face like a veil, but not before Dwight saw her blue-green eyes blur. She shifted on the window ledge and stared out across the field with her back to them.

A lovely woman trying to hold back tears made Dwight as uncomfortable as any man.

"We'll find out," he promised. "It takes time, but we're getting closer every day. That's really what I stopped by to tell you. I spent the morning up at the airport and it looks awfully much like Bernie Covington was out here when Jake was killed. I don't have proof that he shot Jake, but he *was* here."

Her emotions under control again, Kate swung around to listen.

"He rented a car at the airport that Friday before Jake was shot and returned it that same Sunday night.

Paid cash each time. The charge card he used for ID
was phony, by the way. The address he used, too. The
company doesn't have any records of a Charles Bernard, so they can't help us. I was really counting on
that to give us an idea of where Covington's been since
last fall and what he was up to.

"All we know for sure is that he was in Mexico
about the time James Tyrrell drowned and that he was
here in North Carolina when Jake got shot."

"And then back to Mexico," said Kate, puzzled.
"Isn't that what you said yesterday—that Bernie Covington was seen in Costa Verde a month or so *after* the
boating accident?"

"That's right. And I talked to the airlines that had
flights heading south that Sunday night. It's just amaz-
ing what those people can pull out of their computers
these days! One of those passenger lists for October 9
showed a Charles Bernard routed as far as Brownsville,
Texas. From there, it's just a hop, skip, and a jump
down the coast to Costa Verde."

"Why'd he want to go back down yonder for?" asked
Bessie.

"We don't know yet."

"What about incoming flights for this trip?" Kate
asked.

"No luck," said Dwight. "They punched in the
names Bernard and Covington, but nothing useful came
up on the screens. He could've flown in from anywhere
and, of course, he could've used a different name altogether. You don't have to show any ID to buy a plane
ticket."

"Mexico in September," Kate mused. "Up to North
Carolina and back to Mexico in October, then here
again in March to get himself killed."

"I just bet he was the one that stole Mr. James's
stuff out of Gilead's attic," said Bessie. "Stole 'em in
October and come back for Jake's things, only this time
that Kid was waiting for him and killed him dead."

Her theory sounded plausible to Kate. "So now the
Kid—William Thompson?—could still be roaming

around the area? Why, why, *why?*" There was pain and frustration in Kate's voice. "What's here for him?"

Dwight shrugged. "Maybe Covington stashed something here that he needs before he can move on. Maybe he's broke right now until he can find it."

"So he's stolen Sally Whitley's earrings, risked getting caught here where it could do him the most harm, merely so he'd have something to hock for food or traveling money?" Kate frowned. "Sounds rather stupid to me."

"Criminals aren't always known for their smarts," Dwight told her.

"May not be too smart, but he's sure got everybody flummoxed," Bessie said dryly. "And where's he holed up to do all this, Dwight? Ain't nobody seen strangers 'round here. Kate, you and Mr. Gordon walk all over both places. Y'all seen any sign of extra boot tracks? Has Tucker Sauls or Mr. Lacy? Willy sure ain't and he asked up at the store, too."

She presented a strong argument, thought Dwight. To his way of thinking, a farmer was the most territorial creature going and exceedingly jealous of all unauthorized impingements. A farmer will share his watermelons or sweet corn, invite you to help yourself to a bushel of peas, or help you dig wild dogwoods in his woods to transplant to your lawn; but pick even a dandelion from his fence row without permission and his hackles begin to rise. He lives in such intimacy with the land inside his boundaries that he almost knows when a blade of grass or grain of sand has been disturbed.

Even if William Thompson could live totally on the land, someone would have heard a rifle shot, would have noticed a campfire, or seen one of the hundred other signs a human forager cannot help leaving. In the thickest woods, along a deserted stretch of creek, a woods-smart interloper might escape attention for a week or so, but moving back and forth for three weeks?

Not hardly likely, thought Dwight.

"I don't suppose you've remembered something

Jake ever mentioned about Vietnam that would help us?" he asked Kate.

She shook her head. "Nothing. It was so long before we met, and even the few times that he and James got together, there was none of that remember-the-good-old-war-days. At least not that I heard. They felt lucky to get out alive and they just didn't talk about it."

" 'The few times they got together'?" asked Dwight. "I thought they were right good friends."

"They were. What they went through together forged a bond that could never be broken; but after college, Jake got caught up in his career and later we were married. James was sort of drifting along with Gordon and Elaine and he never married, so as time passed, he and Jake had less and less in common. But even though they didn't see each other much anymore, I think Jake still considered James his closest male friend, and if James had ever needed his help, Jake would have dropped everything to give it.

"But so far as sharing any war secrets—" Kate spread her hands helplessly. "I just don't know."

"Don't worry. Sooner or later, we'll get a line on William Thompson and everything will fall into place. I'll keep you informed."

He swung himself down from the counter to leave and snagged a couple of Bessie's oatmeal cookies in passing.

"Two for the road," he told her with the same easy grin that had got 'round her in his high school days. "Y'all take care, hear?"

"That Dwight, he don't change a lick," Bessie said when he'd gone; and while she helped unpack Kate's art books, she related some of Dwight's on- and off-court antics. Of his current domestic problems though, she was silent except to remark when Kate alluded to them, "That Jonna ain't got the sense God gave a turnip. You want me to help you get another load of boxes?"

"No, thanks, Bessie. You've done enough for one day. Come on and I'll drive you home. We'll stop at the house and I'll give you a check for the cushion material now."

"No hurry on that," Bessie protested; but Kate insisted she'd forget if she let it go, so Bessie waited in the car while Kate ran in for her checkbook.

"I'm going on up to the store," Kate said as she pulled into Bessie's driveway and came to a stop under a pear tree in full bloom by the back porch. "Want me to pick anything up for you?"

"Well, it'd save a trip if you'd bring me some drinks. Wait a minute and I'll get the bottles."

While Kate waited, Willy Stewart rumbled up from the field on his huge green tractor. He parked it at the edge of the yard and climbed down with steady deliberation.

Kate opened her car door and got out. "Hi, Willy," she called.

"Afternoon, Miss Kate," he said, removing a straw hat bleached by the sun and stained with his sweat. "How you been keeping these days?"

Willy Stewart retained the old-fashioned courtesies of a southern black man. Although Kate had asked him to drop the "Miss," such familiarity made him uncomfortable. Unless she was blood kin, Willy was constitutionally unable to call any female over the age of twelve, black or white, anything except "Miss" or "Aunt" and Kate had quit trying to change him.

"I'm doing fine, Willy. How about you?"

"Fine, fine. I got no complaints."

"You sure?" she teased. "Your Wolfpack wasn't very fierce this year, I hear."

"More like puppydogs than wolves, won't they?" Willy said gamely. "I reckon God didn't want us to get too prideful. But we won last year and Coach V'll bring 'em 'round again."

It sounded like wishful thinking to Kate and she changed the subject to the pear blossoms drifting down around them.

"Yeah, I think it's gonna be a right good fruit year," Willy said, and they walked over to look at an early plum that had already begun to set fruits.

Although most deciduous trees were leafing out now, Kate noticed that a large one out by the tractor shelter showed no signs of life. "Looks like you've lost that tree," she said.

"No, black walnuts be like crepe myrtles," he told her. "Last to get their leaves in spring."

Bessie appeared on the back porch. She apologized to Kate for taking so long to bring out the bottles and fussed at Willy because he hadn't put the last one back in the carton and she'd had to hunt for where he'd left it by his recliner at lunchtime.

"It's all right," said Kate. "I'm not punching a time clock."

She stuck the bottles in her car and drove out to the paved road, then on up to the crossroads store.

At that time of day, the little country grocery was deserted except for Mrs. Fowler, who was watching a televised game show, and a stiff-legged yellow dog that stood up and growled when Kate entered.

"Oh, be quiet!" shushed Mrs. Fowler and, seeing Kate hesitate in the doorway, she added scornfully, "Don't worry about *him*. He won't bite biscuits."

His act blown, the dog lay back down, flopped its thin tail on the wide-planked floor, and closed its eyes.

"He could have fooled me," Kate laughed.

She put Bessie's empty bottles in a wooden crate and refilled the carton with cold soft drinks from an ancient refrigerated chest that still used chunks of floating ice to chill the bottles. She added orange juice for herself and handed over cash for her purchases.

"Looks like that baby's growing fine," said Mrs. Fowler, ringing up the sale. "Bet you feel better now that you've gone to maternity clothes."

"I do," Kate said. She opened her checkbook. "I finally remembered to bring this. What did you say Mr. Lacy's tab was again? Three hundred-forty-something?"

Mrs. Fowler looked confused, then her plump face cleared. "Oh, he paid up Saturday."

"He did?"

"Sure did. Cash on the barrelhead off a roll that

looked like he'd just come from an upstalk tobacco market. I told him did he hit the jackpot at Atlantic City and he said no, he'd gone and married a rich old widow woman for her money. That Mr. Lacy! He's sure something else, isn't he?"

Kate closed her checkbook and agreed that Lacy Honeycutt sure was something else.

Chapter Nineteen

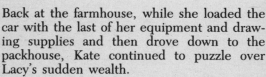

Back at the farmhouse, while she loaded the car with the last of her equipment and drawing supplies and then drove down to the packhouse, Kate continued to puzzle over Lacy's sudden wealth.

It just didn't add up. Lacy with a large bankroll? She knew he and Tucker Sauls hadn't cut that many trees. Two or three cords of firewood sold, and perhaps two truckloads of logs that were sound enough to saw into a few thousand board feet of planks or two-by-fours. Surely that could add up to no more than four or five hundred dollars. And since Tucker Sauls was going halves, Lacy shouldn't have cleared more than two-fifty or three hundred for himself. Yet somehow he'd bought a set of new tires for his truck and settled his account with Mrs. Fowler.

From a very fat wallet if Mrs. Fowler could be believed.

•   •   •

Mary Pat and Aunt Susie were waiting for her on the top step of the packhouse when Kate eased the car down the rutted lane and backed it up to the door.

"I passed your kittens in the lane," Kate said, noting the crumpled grocery bag the child was holding. She often brought bones and scraps from Gilead's kitchen to feed the cats and dogs.

The little girl stood on tiptoes to open the door for Kate, who tried not to step on the old beagle as she negotiated the steps with a bulky set of large drawing pads.

"I could help you carry stuff in."

"That would be nice," Kate said.

Mary Pat was young, but she managed the smaller boxes and proved quite helpful at several simple tasks. She arranged the tiny bottles of Winsor and Newton inks by label color, shelved books, and put sharp points on the colored pencils with Kate's electric pencil trimmer. She separated paper clips and pen nibs from rubber bands and gum erasers, and took time off to spell out her name in pushpins on the new corkboard, chattering all the time about kittens, the new sneakers she and Sally were to shop for tomorrow, and how mean somebody was to take Sally's earrings when he wasn't supposed to.

Kate listened with only half an ear; and by the time Tom Whitley arrived in the late afternoon with the exterior paint, almost everything was neatly stowed away.

"If the fluorescent lights were connected, I could start work tonight," she told Tom happily.

"Let me see what I can do about that," said Tom.

He brought his toolbox in from the truck and pulled out pliers and nippers with insulated handles. As he lifted the trapdoor to go down into the pit where the fusebox was located, Kate said, "Is Sally still upset about the earrings?"

Tom looked at her blankly. "Earrings?"

"Didn't you stop by Gilead before you came here?"

"No, why?" He let the trapdoor drop with a heavy thud. "What's happened? Is Sally okay?"

"She's fine," Kate assured him. "Well, no, not fine exactly, but not physically hurt."

She was startled by the abruptness of his sudden change. From shy and soft-spoken, Tom Whitley turned into a white-faced, clench-jawed fury who grasped her arm and demanded, "What's happened, dammit?"

"Honestly, Tom, she's all right," said Kate, pulling away from his bruising touch. "Someone ransacked your rooms after lunch and took some earrings that were Sally's mother's, but she's—"

"The filthy bastard!" Tom's voice was thick with venomous anger. He slammed out to his truck, jerked it into gear, and dug off up the lane.

"Maybe I'd better go home, too," said Mary Pat in a small voice, and edged toward the door.

"Wait a minute and I'll drive you," said Kate. She closed the windows, shooed the cats and Aunt Susie outside, and turned the key in the new lock Tom Whitley had installed.

Mary Pat was silent as they drove up the lane and Kate was concerned.

"When you love somebody the way Tom loves Sally, you don't want her to get hurt," she told her small cousin. "Tom shouldn't have flown off the handle, but he was angry because somebody made Sally sad."

"Maybe that wasn't really Tom," said Mary Pat, her face to the window.

"Of course it was Tom. People don't stop being themselves just because they get angry, sweetheart. Anyhow, Tom'll calm down as soon as he sees that Sally's okay."

Mary Pat didn't argue, but Kate saw her shoulder lift in a barely perceptible shrug.

Gordon was standing by the study door as Kate slowed to a stop and he came out to meet them. Mary Pat hopped from the car and slipped past him without speaking.

"Something wrong?" he asked Kate.

"Not really." She put the car in neutral, but did not switch it off. "Tom got rather emotional when he heard about the theft and I think it upset Mary Pat a little."

Gordon turned with a worried expression. "Perhaps I'd better talk to her. Come on in, Kate. I won't be long."

"No, I can't stay. Rob Bryant said he was going to bring dinner a little later. I just want to look at your woodpile if I might?"

"Woodpile?"

"The firewood you bought from Lacy. Two cords, wasn't it?"

"That's right. Why?"

"No reason exactly," Kate hedged.

"Is this a variation on dill pickles and strawberry ice cream?" Gordon asked, half-curious, half-amused.

"Probably. Humor me, please, Gordon, and tell me how much you paid Lacy for the wood?"

"Eighty dollars a cord, delivered and stacked," Gordon said promptly. "It's in the shelter back of the garage. Want me to come show you?"

"Thanks, but I'll find it. You go see about Mary Pat."

"Okay." He paused. "Think you'll be free to walk tomorrow?"

"Probably." She shifted into low gear.

The wide drive split at the rear of the house. Half went to the four-car garage, the other circled behind the utility buildings and led between woods and fields to the Gilbert family graveyard some distance back. Kate drove around to the woodshed and cut her motor.

She spent several minutes examining the wood while the sun dipped toward the western trees and the warm air began to cool. Pine and oak she readily identified. Pine beetles could still be heard gnawing away and she could see that the oak centers were spongy. There was some twisted hickory and some of that tulip poplar that had been struck by lightning last summer. Nothing else.

Thoughtfully, Kate drove back to the farm and examined Lacy's neatly stacked firewood. More of the same.

What she sought wasn't there.

She walked into the empty house and pulled one of the insect books from the shelf. This time, she paid attention to what she read.

Her anger was tempered with regret by the time she closed the book and looked at her watch. Six o'clock. No point trying to call the State Forestry Division, she decided, leafing through the telephone directory, but State University probably held evening classes.

She dialed and eventually got through to an assistant professor in the forestry department, who listened to her questions and then earnestly apologized for not knowing the precise answer.

"Dr. Lee's the man you want to talk to," he said. "All I could give you is a ballpark estimate."

"That's good enough," Kate told him.

In less enlightened parts of the United States, "barbecue" is a verb. In eastern North Carolina, though, Kate had quickly learned that the word is always a noun, occasionally modified by the adjective "pork" for the benefit of outsiders.

Much newspaper ink has been devoted to the identification of the best barbecue house in the area—letters to the editor regularly erupt on the subject—but purists agree that authentic barbecue begins with a whole pig split lengthways, cooked slowly all night over a bed of hickory and charcoal, then chopped and seasoned with a judicious mixture of vinegar, salt, red pepper, brown sugar, and Tabasco. The proportions may vary from chef to chef, but tomato in any form is never an ingredient. Never, *ever*.

Traditionalists serve pork barbecue with coleslaw, hot and crusty hush puppies and the inevitable iced tea; but when Rob Bryant returned promptly as promised at six-thirty with a large paper bag that emitted entrancing aromas to Kate's hungry nose, he had thoughtfully substituted a cold six-pack of imported ale.

He had also brought Miss Emily, who bounced in wearing a pink and green plaid skirt topped with a pink sweater set.

"Guess who invited herself to dinner, too?" he asked.

"Hello, Kate, dear," said Miss Emily, reaching up to give Kate a hug before she began setting out the various cartons of food.

Rob kept extra clothes at his mother's house and he had changed from his lawyer's uniform of tailored gray suit and buttoned-down shirt to a pair of comfortable chinos, loafers, and a baggy rust-colored sweater that almost matched the color of his hair.

"It's a fine thing," he complained with mock severity, "when a man can't have dinner with someone without his mother horning in."

"Oh, hush fussing," said his parent, confident of her welcome. "You bought enough barbecue to feed Sherman's army and besides, it's not like you and Kate are courting or anything."

There was an immediate and highly self-conscious moment of complete silence. Miss Emily's prattling, innocent tongue went speechless with surprised awareness as she watched her younger son's face flame redder than the sunset to be seen through the kitchen windows.

After a day of tension and downright melodrama, Kate was back in a happy mood and, misreading Rob's discomfort, she teased, "How *would* you come courting me, Cousin Robbie? Would you wine me on moonshine and dine me on fatback?"

"Shucks, ma'am. Ain't nothin' fine enough fer you 'cepting a nice mess of collard greens and chit'lings," Rob drawled.

"*Anyhow,*" said Miss Emily with a flustered air, "I'm here to balance the table, so where's that Lacy?"

"I've no idea," said Kate, "but he usually shows up in time for supper."

They set four places at the table, but began without Lacy since there was no telling when he'd return and "hush puppies wait for no man," said Rob, who knew by long experience that cold cornbread wasn't worth putting on one's plate.

The evening was still warm and Kate had left the heavy wooden door open with only the screen door to keep out early-flying moths. As darkness fell and spring peepers tuned up in the bottom, the kitchen became lively with talk and laughter.

All self-consciousness was gone as Kate and Rob interrupted each other to tell Miss Emily of how Bessie had rescued the snake from shotgun and hoe earlier in the day; and Miss Emily described the time she'd accidentally picked up a copperhead the first year she helped Rob's father weed the tobacco plantbed.

"I slung that thing halfway across Colleton County," she said, shuddering in memory. "And I trampled so many plants getting out of the bed that your daddy had to borrow some from Andrew Honeycutt to finish setting out his last field."

Rob topped their glasses with rich amber ale. "Did you ever tell Kate about the year Jerry Chifton brought a pregnant garter snake to school for a science project—"

"—and we wound up with baby snakes in every corner of the building," Miss Emily finished for him. "You wouldn't believe how many babies one little old garter snake could hold, Kate! And of course, you know how silly teenage girls can be. They started screaming every time they even saw a pencil on the floor, thinking it was another snake. They were in the teachers' lounge, in the lunchroom—I still think some of those senior boys might have been bringing extras from home 'cause I know for a fact that the one that showed up in the county supervisor's briefcase was bigger than the other babies."

Her plump little face took on a look of determination. "That class'll be having its fifteenth reunion in May and I don't care if he *is* a preacher now, I'm going to make Curtis Sorrell admit he's the rascal that put one in my desk drawer."

Lacy's old pickup had rattled into the yard as she talked and soon Lacy himself appeared at the screen door. He blinked in the bright light and something about the way he hesitated just beyond the threshold made Kate's anger at him do another flip-flop because she realized how the room must look to him—dinner in progress, three people in warm companionship and easy chatter, and he the outsider now that Jake was gone.

"There you are, Lacy!" exclaimed Miss Emily. "If you don't hurry up, we're going to eat all your supper."

"I ain't 'specially hungry," said Lacy, hanging his denim jacket and felt hat behind the door. He washed his hands at the sink and came to the table slowly, smoothing his thin white hair with one hand and brushing at his overalls with the other, and awkwardly took his place between the two women.

Why, he's actually shy, thought Kate, and handed the old farmer the bowl of chopped barbecue with a kindlier air than she could have managed an hour ago.

Accustomed to his taciturnity, Miss Emily retold her copperhead-in-the-plantbed story and chattered and charmed until Lacy loosened up enough to recall a hot summer day some two or three years ago when he and Jake went swimming in the creek and a cottonmouth water moccasin decided to join them.

"It musta been stretched out on a tree limb we was wading under 'cause all of a sudden, *kerplop!* There it was, right in the water between us. We was halfway through the woods 'fore either one of us missed our pants."

It was a story Kate had heard from Jake.

"With all the jogging I do, I thought I was in pretty good shape," he had told her, "but Lacy's skinny shanks stayed five yards ahead of me all the way."

And she had laughed at the picture the two men must have made, erupting out of the creek, mother-naked, to scandalize two respectable black women who had been fishing quietly upstream.

"I don't know if it's safe to let you loose in the country anymore," she had told him, standing in their apartment by the long windows that overlooked the river.

Back then, it was the city that had seemed dangerous to her, not the country's natural perils. She was not athletic and it had worried her that he ran alone through empty early morning streets. Except in hunting season, she had never felt such apprehension about Jake's quick trips to the farm.

"Lacy gets lonesome," he used to say when the weeks in New York stretched out too long.

"Who gets lonesome?" she teased, for by then they had been married long enough that she knew his needs.

In those years, Jake wanted the city's jostling, rough competition. Too long in the country made him as edgy as too long in town. The farm was quiet, *too* quiet, and too familiar for challenge; but Kate had expected the pattern to reverse some day, that their visits would become more frequent and, eventually, would lengthen into residence. She had thought they would grow old there together, tottering back to the city only for special occasions, to see a favorite actor or visit old colleagues.

Neither she nor Jake had ever expected that she would live here without him, alone except for an embittered old man.

Lacy reached for a hush puppy and Kate saw with new clarity his callused wrinkled hand, his bony wrist extended past the worn cuff of his flannel work shirt. The ale and the laughter had relaxed his defenses and she read fatigue in the lines of his face, in the slump of his shoulders. Whatever he was up to, it was taking a physical toll.

He's too old for this, Kate thought. He's Jake's *uncle*, the nearest thing to a grandfather your baby will ever have.

He stole, said another, colder part of her.

He *took*, she corrected, and no more than Jake would have given if Jake had realized.

Impulsively, she laid down her fork and said, "Before you finish settling Jake's estate, Rob, I'd like you to transfer half those CDs to Lacy."

As soon as the words were out of her mouth, Kate wished she had waited. She should have known that Miss Emily would start beaming and burbling about generosity and that Lacy's pride would be stung by anything smacking of self-serving charity.

"What's a ceedee?" he asked Rob. "Money? I ain't having none of her money." His voice was harsh.

"Lacy, please don't do this," she begged and stretched her hand toward his.

His chair scraped the floor as he shoved himself out of reach, as if her very touch were poison.

"I don't need her to give me no money."

"You'd rather steal it?" Kate asked caustically.

"Now, Kate," said Rob, but his mother laid a restraining hand on his arm.

Kate didn't notice.

"Since when do pine borers attack black walnuts, Lacy?" she asked and anger reddened her thin cheeks. "There was nothing wrong with those trees, was there? They weren't dead, they just hadn't leafed out yet. How much did you and Sauls get for each one? Four hundred? Five?"

Miss Emily couldn't help herself. "Five hundred dollars for one tree?"

"I talked to a forestry expert this evening," Kate told her. "That's the approximate going rate for standing furniture-quality black walnut trees around here. And Lacy and his crony cut six of them."

"My daddy planted them trees," said Lacy.

"Your daddy was Jake's grandfather. Those trees belonged to Jake," Kate blazed. "You had no right to steal them from Jake's child!"

"It ain't Jake's!" howled Lacy. "Jake woulda told me iffen he was gonna be a daddy."

Kate was stunned. "He didn't know. It was too soon."

"Huh!" snarled Lacy. "He didn't know 'cause it weren't his. Then you come running down here to hide your shame from your New York City friends, making everybody here feel sorry for you, thinking it's Jake's baby; but I heared you talking on the telephone to him."

"Him? Him who?" asked Kate, bewildered.

"Your *parrymore*, that's who. That Richard that called you up." Lacy's harsh voice became mincing as he tried to imitate Kate's. " 'Oh, Richard, darling, I'm just missing you so much, but I've got to have our baby down here.' And every time you talk to that Gina woman, it's 'Give my love to Richard.' "

"Richard? *Richard Cromyn?*"

Kate's mind went back to that call she'd had from her old friend at the agency two weeks ago. She could remember the silly banter between them and tried to recall how it must have sounded to Lacy's suspicious ears. "You thought that Richard and I—? Oh, for God's sake, Lacy!"

She turned to Rob. "You've met Richard Cromyn, Rob. Will you please tell Lacy how stupid he's being?"

Rob's green eyes shone with mischief. "Is Cromyn that old guy who—"

At Kate's confirming nod, he shook his head at the bristling old farmer who stood across the table from him and said, "Sorry, Mr. Lacy. Not only is Richard Cromyn thirty years older than Kate, I think he's been completely faithful to the same man for the last fifteen."

Rob spoke with such humorous conviction that Lacy's belligerence faltered. "It really *is* Jake's baby?"

He looked around the table at Miss Emily, at Rob, and at last he came to Kate. Her eyes were chips of blue-green glass and his angular chin tightened convulsively. "I didn't— I thought—"

His words died and he made blindly for the hall door and they heard his footsteps stumble up the stairs.

Rob started to follow, but his mother called him back.

"Leave him alone," she said with the sharpness of a school principal. "It's about time Lacy Honeycutt took a good look at himself for once."

As reaction set in, Kate hugged herself bleakly, feeling as stripped and desolate as on the day of Jake's funeral. "How could he think that? Didn't he know how

Jake and I—? Did he think I could go to another man that quickly?"

She shivered and helpless tears spilled down her face.

Rob ached to put his arms around her, but he was realistic enough to know how she would react to that now, and anyhow, his mother was already there, hugging and patting Kate's hunched shoulders.

"He wasn't thinking, child," she said. "He was just hurting."

Unable to go on standing by uselessly, Rob cleared the table and carried the scraps out to the dogs. He sat on the edge of the porch in darkness and fed cold hush puppies to the two pointers who'd temporarily given up their romantic siege of Willy Stewart's dog pen. Jake's porch, he thought. Jake's farm and Jake's pointers.

And Jake's wife.

There had been too much difference in their ages when they were growing up, but Jake had been tolerant of Rob's hero worship and let him tag along occasionally when Dwight would have left him behind. They became friends after Jake came back from Vietnam and both were in school over at Chapel Hill. And Jake had enjoyed the joke when Rob claimed his brand-new wife as a distant cousin.

"Just as long as you don't try to pretend you're kissing cousins," he'd warned and there had been a sardonic, speculative look in his hazel eyes that still made Rob flush to remember.

When Rob returned to the kitchen, the big room was deserted and he heard the murmur of his mother's voice from Kate's bedroom down the hall. He stowed the rest of the barbecue and coleslaw in the refrigerator, pushed up the sleeves of his baggy sweater and washed the few dishes they had used.

Miss Emily joined him at the sink in time to dry the final plate. "I put her to bed."

"Is she okay?"

"She'll be fine." Her worried eyes peered up at him. "Will you?"

He knew it was no use pretending not to know what she was talking about.

Chapter
Twenty

 When Miss Emily coaxed her to bed the night before, Kate had expected to lie awake until the small hours deciding what to do since it was clear she could no longer stay at the farm in the face of Lacy's monstrous distaste for her presence. But after such draining emotion, she had fallen into a deep sleep untroubled by dreams or nightmares, and she awoke shortly before daybreak feeling rested and even somewhat hopeful.

It was still so early that dawn was only a rumor in the eastern sky. The old moon, a lopsided and cold white fourth quarter now, lit up the countryside; and looking from her open windows past the yard trees, Kate saw ground mist lying across the sloping fields, making the woods beyond seem to float untethered in the distance. Details were obscured and the luminous beauty of the scene recalled Chinese brush paintings of misty moonlit landscapes.

From the chicken yard, Lacy's rooster proclaimed

the coming sun, and wild birds were equally noisy. Bobwhites and towhees called to each other and a Carolina wren rustled busily in the dead grass beneath her window with much chirping and quick flicks of its stubby little tail. In Miss Emily's pasture across the road, cows mooed for their breakfast hay.

The air that floated through the windows was cool and invigorating, with a blend of clean country smells: crab apple blossoms, hyacinths, dew-wet grass, and freshly turned earth. It stirred Kate's blood and she threw off her robe and hastily dressed in elasticized jeans and an oversized cherry-colored sweatshirt. She planned to grab some cheese and a piece of fruit and be out of the house before Lacy stirred.

But the aroma of fresh coffee met her in the hallway, and when she reached the kitchen, she found Lacy at the table laboring with pencil and paper. He crumpled the page as she entered.

"I meant to be gone 'fore you got up," he said, and pushed a small sheaf of currency across the polished tabletop toward her. "This is what's left outten them walnut trees. I'll try and have you the rest by the end of summer."

Kate was embarrassed by his hangdog look. "Oh, Lacy—"

"I can stay with Tucker for right now and work at the sawmill till barning time," he continued doggedly.

"Don't be silly. If one of us has to leave, it ought to be me. What do I know about chickens and pigs and gardens and tobacco allotments? Not to mention borer beetles?" she added wickedly.

But Lacy was in full contrition this morning and would not be baited. "Looks like you'll just have to learn," he said with the mildness of a Sunday school saint. "It ain't fitting for me to stay on here after what I done and what I said about you."

"Yeah, that was pretty rotten," Kate agreed. She poured herself a coffee and refilled Lacy's cup, too, before he could refuse. Then she sat down across from him with determination and said, "Look, Lacy, it's time we got this settled. You've never liked me and I can't say I've been overly crazy about you. We tolerated each other though because of Jake, right?"

He looked at her warily, then nodded slowly.

"So why can't we keep on like that? We both loved Jake, but he wasn't perfect. In fact, in one thing he was downright selfish and thoughtless."

Lacy's head jerked up defensively, but Kate did not pause.

"Jake wanted to have his cake and eat it, too. I didn't keep him in the city, Lacy. He kept himself there. He loved his work. But he loved the farm, too, and he wanted it to stay just the way it was when he was a boy—dogs, chickens, pigs, his hunting guns oiled and ready, a bed waiting for him, one of your home-cooked meals on the stove. He wanted the orchard pruned in the fall and the grass cut in summer."

"He pruned them pear trees hisself," Lacy objected hotly.

"Okay," she conceded, "so he did some of the work himself, but that was still weekend play. It relaxed him. And if he hadn't felt like doing it, you would have, right?"

Lacy would not respond.

"Lacy, it's not disloyal to admit Jake was wrong. I know he took care of your tab at the feed store and at Mrs. Fowler's, and he had all the utility bills sent to New York, but he should have been paying you a real salary all those years."

"You don't pay kinfolk no salary."

"I don't see why not."

"That's 'cause you're a Yankee," he said scornfully.

"Damn it, Lacy! Taking advantage of a relative has nothing to do with the Mason-Dixon line. If you hadn't been here to look after the farm for Jake, how much would he have had to pay a caretaker?"

Lacy's jaw set mulishly.

"Okay," said Kate, shifting tactics. "So you're going to leave me here to fend for myself while Jake's murderer roams the countryside. How would Jake like that?"

"I could maybe find somebody to stay here with you and do the chores."

"Oh, sure. You think I'm going to give a stranger your room at a time like this?"

Lacy's eyes dropped to the bulge outlined by her cherry-colored sweatshirt. "Well, maybe I could stay on till you—till after the baby—"

"Your great-nephew, Lacy," she reminded in her softest voice. "Or great-niece. Your blood kin."

Silence stretched between them. The first rays of sunlight edged in through the eastern windows and made patterns on the tabletop.

"Jake were a real easy baby," Lacy mused, half to himself. "Only time he ever cried much was with the colic once and Jane was so plumb wore-out I took him out on the porch swing with me and laid him on my chest and we swung back and forth till he went to sleep."

"Now see there?" smiled Kate. "I was never around a baby before, so you could tell me what's normal and what's not when it cries."

"I reckon you'll get all the advice you need from Em'ly Bryant and Bessie Stewart," Lacy said dryly. "Them two's the buttingest-in women I ever seen."

Kate laughed. "In the meantime, you'd better keep this," she said, pushing the money back to Lacy.

He started to protest, but she said, "You and I aren't blood kin, Lacy, so it's only right that you should've been getting a salary since last October and I don't want any more fuss about it." She stood up briskly. "I don't think it's good for the baby for me to argue so much."

Lacy snorted, but he pocketed the money and pushed back his chair. "Reckon I'd better go see if them chickens has us some fresh eggs."

Chapter
Twenty-One

 It was, thought Kate, walking down to the new studio after lunch, rather like living on the edge of a volcano. A volcano that could erupt again at any time.

Jake was murdered. Of this she had no doubts. And Jake's army comrade, Bernie Covington, had been struck down here in this very packhouse. The boating mishap that killed James Tyrrell seemed too fortuitous not to be murder cleverly disguised as an accident, and whoever was responsible—William Thompson?—was still running loose, walking in and out of Gilead and the Honeycutt farmhouse at will.

Yet, now that she had made peace with Lacy, she could begin to plan for the future, to think about work and new projects to discuss with Gina Melnick.

It would seem that life went on, even on the edge of a volcano.

It would also seem that settling into a new studio was much like a shakedown cruise aboard a boat. She discovered that the drafting table would work better shifted slightly to the left, that tubes of pastels would be handier in an upper drawer, that mixing trays should be nearer the sink.

As Kate rearranged supplies in a lower cabinet, she noticed an unfamiliar object shoved to the back of the bottom shelf. There was no memory of the crumpled grocery bag Mary Pat had carried the afternoon before, only puzzlement while she crouched on one knee to fish it out from behind a stack of blotting paper.

Wild surmises rioted in her head when she saw the domed cedar box. James Tyrrell's chest? Here?

She lifted the lid upon an assortment of keepsakes very similar to those Jake had saved: bits of papers, letters, a torn map, and a clutch of photographs. Some were duplicates of the ones Jake had. Others showed jungle scenes, temples, marketplaces, unfamiliar trees and flowers: the sort of pictures an ordinary tourist might take. In the black and white snapshots, the men's camouflage uniforms could almost pass for brightly-colored holiday patterns.

There was Jake, barely recognizable behind what looked like a four-day growth of beard, and James Tyrrell in an unkempt mustache beside him. There was Bernie Covington in an enormous black beard that did not obscure the dark mole on his cheek. To his left was the sharply-focused face of William Thompson.

Kate was shocked by how young he looked. No wonder he'd been called Kid. Jake said he had lied about his age and the lie must have been a whopper because this boy—this baby, actually—couldn't have been more than fifteen or sixteen.

Kate turned the picture over and read the scrawled names: "Jake, Bernie, Willie, and me."

Willie Thompson.

Into her mind, unbidden, came the name *Tom Whitley*.

What had Dwight said about criminals taking simple sound-alike aliases and often reversing initials?

Willie Thompson, Thomas Whitley?

Was it possible?

The boy in the photograph was as slightly built as Tom, but he was looking straight into the camera and it was difficult to judge if his chin jutted or receded, if his nose was aquiline or snubbed, if his Adam's apple was prominent or barely noticeable. The longer Kate looked, though, the surer she grew that this was a picture of Tom Whitley.

She was startled from her speculations by the rap of Gordon's walking stick at the open door.

"Ready to walk, Kate?" he called.

"Oh, Gordon, look what I found—James's missing chest!"

"*What?*" Gordon was dumbfounded. "How on earth did that get *here?*"

Kate stared at him blankly. "Do you know, I was so busy looking at the pictures, I never gave it a thought. Look at this, though."

She stabbed the baby face with a slender forefinger. "Who does that remind you of?"

Gordon peered at the figure uncertainly. "He looks familiar."

"Tom Whitley," she prompted.

"Whitley? Really?" He turned the pictures to the north window and examined them so intently and for so long that Kate prodded him impatiently.

"Well? What do you think?"

"It could be, but that would mean—"

Kate nodded excitedly. "We were all wondering how a stranger like William Thompson could walk in and out of our houses, how he could roam around both farms unseen, and here he was under our noses the whole time. Lacy said his set of Vietnam pictures disappeared after he'd shown them to Mary Pat and Sally, remember? Sally or Mary Pat must have mentioned them to Tom. He was here when I unpacked Jake's things, and heaven knows he had free access to Gilead's attic. He must have worried that we'd notice he was one of the four. I wonder if Sally suspects? She said he was in Vietnam."

"But, Kate—"

"We'll have to ask Rob again exactly when he hired Tom," she interrupted. "I wish I could remember what he said the other day about not going through the college. The first caretaker quit or something and Tom's supposed to have heard about Gilead from him. That was after school started, though, which means sometime later in September. After your accident."

Her brow furrowed as she tried to keep the times straight in her mind. "Everything falls into place, Gordon! He could have been in Costa Verde in time to damage the boat somehow. Yes! And Covington saw him or helped him and then came up this month to blackmail him and was killed, only . . ."

"Only what?"

"Well," she said slowly. "Dwight Bryant thinks Covington, not Thompson, shot Jake. He can prove that Covington was up here that weekend in October."

"So?"

"So if Covington killed Jake, how could he blackmail Tom? They'd be equally guilty."

"Unless it wasn't blackmail, just a falling out of thieves," Gordon suggested. "Maybe a disagreement over the split of the spoils?"

"But *what* spoils? What did Jake and James have that they wanted? *Think*, Gordon!"

She dumped the contents of the wooden chest on her drawing table. A carved ivory bead rolled off the edge and Gordon bent to pick it up.

As he stretched down, his shirt collar pulled away from the back of his neck to reveal a flat brown mole surmounted by two tiny reddish birthmarks, each no larger than a pinhead.

In a flash of dé jà vu, Kate was transported back to a dinner party at Patricia and Philip Carmichael's penthouse. She could almost hear the murmured small talk and the clink of glasses. Her dinner partner had dropped his fork and, as he leaned over beside her to retrieve it, she had noticed an inconspicuous triad of birthmarks and mole ordinarily hidden by the collar of his shirt.

"James!" she gasped. "You're James!"

He jerked upright and all the color drained from his face. "What are you saying?"

"N-nothing," she stammered, instantly aware of enormous danger. "I thought for a minute—so stupid of me—in this light, you reminded me so much of James. But that's silly. Of course you would. You were brothers."

"Too late, Kate," he said heavily. "I was afraid of this."

He studied her bleakly and regret shadowed his gaze. "We met so few times that I thought you wouldn't know me without my mustache, or that you'd be like all the others and assume I only resembled James because no one here had ever seen Gordon without a beard. What made you suddenly recognize me?"

He doesn't know about the marks on his neck, she thought, and found herself remembering the night Mary Pat lay with her head on his shoulder and sang about a spotted pony. *Mary Pat knew!* That's why she thought things could change overnight. James was in the habit of giving her piggyback rides and she recognized the back of James's neck even though everyone told her this was Uncle Gordon.

"You bastard!" she blurted angrily. "You killed Jake!"

"No!" His hands clenched his ornate walking stick until his knuckles whitened around its heavy carving. "No, that was Bernie, not me. It was all his idea, not mine. You must believe me, Kate. When Rob called me and said Jake was dead—"

There was no mistaking the anguish in his face, but Kate was beyond caring for his pain. "You may not have pulled the trigger, but Jake's dead because he was the one person who would keep you from masquerading here as Gordon. I suppose you killed Elaine and Gordon, too?"

"No, no, *NO!*" he cried. "That's not how it happened. Good God, Kate, what kind of monster do you think I am?"

"I don't know, James. You tell me."

"The boat accident was real," he said earnestly. "The mast snapped in the storm, she took too much water for the pumps to handle and she sank. That's the truth. At least, it's the truth so far as I know. What I said about partial amnesia was true, too. I really don't remember what happened that afternoon. It was days before I began to regain consciousness. I had a severe concussion, my leg was broken, my jaw was broken, too, and wired shut for good measure. I was in and out of a coma for weeks. The doctors and nurses were all Mexican. They told me that my brother and Señora Tyrrell had drowned and that was all. I didn't realize there'd been a mix-up—that they had me on their charts as Gordon—until they let me have visitors and Covington was the first one in. He'd come to offer condolences, I suppose. I could talk a little between clenched teeth, so to speak, and I greeted him familiarly when he walked in."

"So you had been seeing him in Costa Verde before the accident?"

"Oh, yes. We'd kept in touch. In fact, you might even say we were business associates. Bernie was my supplier and we'd done a little dealing."

"Drugs?" Kate was surprised. She'd never associated him with drugs.

"Don't look so shocked. I'm not talking hard-core addicts, just people getting a happy buzz on after dinner. You must have friends who are into recreational drugs. A little coke, a little speed. That's all this was. I didn't let Gordon know because Elaine was straitlaced about drugs, even though this was nothing worse than Lacy and his moonshine that everybody thinks is so cute—just enough to keep my friends happy and give me some extra pocket money."

Kate looked scornful and James shrugged.

"Anyhow, Bernie realized I was James and tumbled to the possibilities immediately. I'd told him about Patricia's will at the time Elaine and Gordon became Mary Pat's guardians, and he was the one who saw that with Gordon dead, I was back out in the cold; but with the authorities thinking it was brother James who had drowned, I could have it all. I told him it was crazy, but he made me promise to think about it."

"And it only took you five minutes to decide," Kate said bitterly.

"As a matter of fact, it was closer to three weeks," he answered quietly. "Bernie trotted out every argument he could think of. You know what finally tipped the balance?"

Kate shook her head.

"Mary Pat. That poor child had seen everybody who ever loved her stripped away, one by one. I had no legal right to her, but I was the only one left who could provide continuity. And by then—" He hesitated and his eyes dropped.

"By then, Jake was dead?" she whispered.

"I had nothing to do with that," he repeated again. "I admit I wanted to pass as Gordon. Hell! Why not? Gordon was dead. Nothing could bring him back, so why should I have thrown away everything without at least considering it? It wasn't as if I were taking anything from Mary Pat. If Gordon had lived, the money would have been his, so what difference did it make if I took his place?

"I honestly didn't think I could pull it off, though. When the bandages came off, I saw they'd shaved my mustache. Covington said that I could blame the accident for any apparent changes and that no one would think twice about Gordon looking like James. They'd put it down to seeing his face without a beard for the first time in twenty years. And it's true that none of Gordon's friends there in Costa Verde was the least suspicious. Jake was the only one I had to worry about."

James's voice slowed as if he was picking his words with care and judging their effect on Kate.

"There was a letter from Jake on my bed when Covington came that Thursday morning. He'd wired condolences earlier, but this was a letter offering to come down to Costa Verde if there was anything he could do to help me. It was a wonderful letter, Kate. He talked about Vietnam and the things we'd done together after we got back to the States. The more I thought about it, the more I knew I couldn't avoid seeing him and he'd know as soon as we met that I wasn't Gordon."

He took a deep breath and looked away from her steady gaze. "I showed Covington the letter. I swear to you, Kate, that I only let him read it to prove how well Jake knew me."

"And Jake had mentioned in the letter that he was coming down to the farm that weekend," she guessed.

"Yes."

In the silence that fell, Kate was wrenched with fresh grief, recalling how stricken Jake had been when he learned that his cousin Elaine and his old friend James had both drowned. He was only waiting to hear that Gordon was out of the hospital and on the mend before he flew down to Costa Verde to offer his sympathy face-to-face.

"If I'd known what Covington was planning, I'd have sent for the doctors right away and told them the truth about who I was. He must have realized I would because he went away before visiting hours were over and he didn't come back all weekend. When Rob called Monday to tell me about Jake, I just lay there stunned. You don't know what a shock it was after losing Gordon and Elaine. Later, I realized that now I *could* be Gordon. I guess I'm not too bright, because it was at least two hours after that before it dawned on me that Jake's hunting accident was just a little too coincidental. When Covington walked into my room Monday night, I took one look at his face and I knew it wasn't a coincidence. I was so damn angry that he'd killed Jake I wanted to call the *policía* and have him lynched."

"But you didn't."

"No. Again, what was the point? Much as I loved Jake—and I *did* love him, Kate—telling wouldn't bring him back, would it?"

"No," she said tonelessly.

"You don't believe me," he sighed. "I can't blame you. But I swore to myself then and there that Bernie Covington was going to pay for Jake's death."

"How very noble. So you brought Mary Pat back to Gilead to play lord of the manor. Why steal those pictures?"

"The wicked flee when no man pursueth, I suppose," he said, with one of his engaging lopsided smiles.

Kate was past being charmed. "You thought someone would recognize you from those old snapshots?"

"I should have left well enough alone," he admitted. "I just don't understand how my chest got here, though. I hid it in an old suitcase up in the attic and the next time I checked, it was gone. I found it in the Whitley bedroom, but the chest wasn't there."

"You were that thief, too? You took Sally's earrings?"

"I had to make it look like a real burglary," he said sheepishly.

"Then someone else knows!"

"Not necessarily. By the time the police came, the suitcase was back in the attic. I'd say it was Sally, only she's as timid as a field mouse."

"She hasn't been here, so it must have been Tom."

"Who cares?" James said impatiently. "Anything he says or does from now on is going to look suspicious."

"You're wrong," she said and pushed away from the drawing table in a rush for the door, but he reached out with his cane and tripped her so that she fell heavily to the floor.

She tried to get up, but James brandished the heavy stick. "Be sensible, Kate," he coaxed.

"What are you going to do?" she asked, sinking back to the floor.

"I don't know yet. I've got to think." His voice broke. "Oh, God, let me *think!*"

"It's all coming apart. There's no way you can kill me and make it look like an accident. Too many people know you're here right now. Lacy knows we were going to take a walk and you must have told someone at Gilead where you would be."

He didn't answer, but she could almost see his brain at work, furiously trying to conjure a scenario that would fit all the details.

"Okay," he said at last, and Kate was chilled by the cold resolution in his tone. "There's no way to keep up the charade, so listen very carefully. I've got to hide you somewhere for a few hours—long enough for me to get to Raleigh and put together some cash and then disappear. I don't want to hurt you, Kate, but I will if you make me."

He searched for a threat that would keep her cooperative. "If you want that baby, you'd better do exactly as I say, because I promise you that if you make me hit you with this stick, I'll aim for the baby first. Do you understand?"

Kate was appalled to realize that he meant it, and she crossed her arms over her abdomen protectively. "I understand," she said shakily.

James scanned the studio until he spotted some electrical flex that Tom had left on a nearby countertop. "Okay, stand up and put your hands behind you," he ordered.

He bound her wrists together tightly and left a length of the plastic-covered wire to act as a leash. From the box of soft rags Kate kept to wipe pens and brushes with, he took strips to act as an eventual gag.

"You're not going to put me in the pit, are you?" she asked fearfully.

"No, they'd find you too fast here."

"Like Bernie Covington?"

"I would have moved him that night, but my leg gave out on me."

"Why did you really kill him? It couldn't have been for Jake's sake. That was five months ago."

"He was getting greedy," James admitted. "He wanted a bigger percentage of Gordon's trust fund than I could spare. I told him to meet me here and we'd discuss it. We'd met here before, so he didn't suspect a thing. I should have loaded his body in his car and left it a hundred miles from here, but I couldn't manage with my leg."

He opened the studio door and took a good look around, but the lane was deserted in both directions and there was no sign of anyone, not even the dogs.

Holding tightly to the electrical cord that bound Kate's wrists, James helped her down the packhouse steps and pointed her toward the row of abandoned tobacco barns. "Down there," he said. "They won't think to look there immediately."

It was only a few hundred feet to the low, tar-paper-covered door and James guided Kate over the step-down threshold to the dirt floor.

The old barn was dank and musty, and ancient cobwebs draped down from the wooden tiers overhead. Ordinarily, light would have filtered through beneath the eaves and air vents under the tin roof, but generations of sparrows had blocked all the spaces with thick straw nests until there was no sunlight or moving air except that which came through the open square door.

James guided Kate to the back of the barn, eased her down onto the damp earth and tied her to one of the wooden tier supports. He was almost gentle as he inserted the gag and left her in the gloomy corner.

He disappeared for several minutes; then, to Kate's horror, returned with a long thin piece of lightwood, the resinous "fatty" heart pine which Lacy often split for kindling.

"Kate, I'm sorry," he apologized. "I can't leave Gilead. You can understand that, can't you? I'm a Tyrrell and a Tyrrell without land is nothing. I'm a good steward, too. How could I give it up?"

Terrified, Kate watched him light the wood with his cigarette lighter.

He lifted the bonnet of the gas burner closest to Kate and holding the torch away, turned the knob.

Nothing happened.

He tried a second burner. "What the devil? I know

there's gas. When I opened the valve on the tank outside, the gauge still registered three-quarters full."

He held the torch closer and saw that the jets were clogged with dirt dauber nests. He banged them sharply and the clay fell away, and a slight hiss of gas could be heard.

Pleased, he moved on to the third burner and repeated the maneuver, explaining as he worked. "I'll jam this torch about halfway up the racks and it'll burn like a candle until enough gas builds up under the rafters. I should have at least three or four hours to establish an alibi. I'll say I came to walk with you, but you weren't at the studio and I went on back to Gilead. By the time a fire truck gets here, it'll be too late and they'll think it was Willie Thompson again. Willie! I wonder where the kid really is now?"

Kate tried to protest through the wad of cloth in her mouth, to reason with him. Only distressed murmurs were audible.

"I wish you wouldn't struggle," he said worriedly. "Please don't. Try to relax. Maybe the gas will put you to sleep first. I wish I didn't have to do this. Oh, God, Kate! Why did you have to recognize me?"

Kate watched helplessly as he approached the fourth and final burner, diagonally opposite from the corner where she was bound. Lying on the dank ground, her view was blocked by the defective burner in front of her. She could only see the top of James's head, the flickering lightwood torch and the shadows it cast on the planked walls.

She heard James tilt back the hood and bang on the jets and she heard the hiss of gas, but there was no way for her to see the semi-comatose corn snake as it writhed from hibernation beneath the burner hood, only inches from James's hand.

James saw the snake's lethargic shape, though, and with an involuntary gesture of revulsion and fear, he jabbed at it with the fiery stick.

The gas ignited in a loud swoosh; then pressure cracked the outdated gas line and the whole burner exploded in a blast that took out the side of the barn behind James.

The explosion sent Kate into darkness as flames raced up the tar-paper siding, devoured the sparrows' straw nests and began in earnest on the wooden structure itself.

Chapter
Twenty-Two

 It was well after midnight before Dwight got back to the hospital and took the elevator to the intensive care unit on the sixth floor.

Even though a hospital is never completely quiet, footsteps are softer along the upper halls late at night, voices are hushed, and the lights are dimmer.

The ICU waiting lounge was nearly empty and the sleepy-eyed volunteer who manned the reception desk looked blank at Dwight's question. "He might have gone down for coffee," she whispered.

At that hour, the only snack bar open in the hospital was a dreary room lined with vending machines on one wall and a row of vinyl-upholstered booths on the other.

Dwight found his brother alone, staring into a foam cup of corrosive-looking black liquid.

"I'd advise against the coffee," Rob said with a weary smile. "It's probably how they keep the beds filled here."

Dwight considered his choices and selected a can of tomato juice. "How are they doing?" he asked as he sat down across from Rob.

"The doctor came by around eight," said Rob, stifling a yawn. "Lacy's burns are pretty superficial. Just his left hand and shoulder where the tier pole hit him. The doctor said it was more of a gash than a burn. They're keeping him overnight for observation because of his age. I went in to see him about ten and they'd given him something to help him sleep."

"What about Kate?"

"They won't let me see her. She's in sterile isolation with second-degree burns on the front of her calves. The doctor says she must have gone into fetal position instinctively to protect the baby. There're first-degree burns on her face, neck and shoulder, and her shoulder was scraped where Lacy wrenched her from under the burner. And a concussion from the blast, of course." He kept his voice steady and unemotional as he catalogued Kate's injuries. "She'll be in a lot of pain when she finally comes to. They're afraid to give her anything too strong because of the baby."

"The baby's okay?"

"Too soon to know. Its heartbeat was too fast. That could be temporary stress. They think so. They hope so." Rob gave a disconsolate shrug. "What about you?"

Dwight thought of all he'd done since the call came in after lunch that one of the Honeycutt barns had exploded in flames. Three people seriously hurt and on their way to Southern Wake, he'd been told, and he had reached the hospital shortly after the rescue ambulance to find Gordon Tyrrell dead on arrival, Kate Honeycutt burned and unconscious, and Lacy Honeycutt hurt and near shock, but lucid.

While the emergency-room staff worked on his wounds, Lacy explained how he'd heard the blast as he was stepping into his old pickup and how he'd driven the truck wide open down the lane to the blazing barn. Gordon's body had been lying across the gaping hole in the side. Flames were everywhere. He'd pulled Gordon free but there was no sign of Kate and she didn't answer when he called, so he'd run around to the back of the barn and jerked open the rear door.

"She was laying on the ground with a burner 'crost her shoulders and I tried to yank her out, but I couldn't budge her and then I seen she was tied to the tier pole with a gag in her mouth and I thought I won't never gonna get her cut loose. That s.o.b. was trying to kill her, Dwight! Why'd he want to do that?"

Across the emergency room on another gurney, Kate writhed in pain just below consciousness. "James," she muttered, as doctors and nurses treated her injuries, ". . . no, James . . . don't . . ."

Dwight had looked at the third gurney then, at the still form abandoned to death, and he began to understand.

"The FBI checked his fingerprints with the army and they confirmed it—he was James, not Gordon." Dwight pulled the tab on the juice can and inserted a straw. "We searched his rooms at Gilead. Had to jimmy the lock on his desk, but we found Sally Whitley's earrings. And Jake's Vietnam things."

"Somehow Kate must have recognized him." Rob rubbed his eyes. They felt bloodshot and full of grit.

"Smart lady," said Dwight, studying his younger brother. It had been a long day for him, but an even longer one for Rob. "You're getting right attached to her, aren't you?"

Rob shot him a wary glance, expecting the needle. It wasn't there.

"You going to marry her?"

"If she'll have me," Rob said humbly.

Dwight finished his juice. "Oh, I imagine she'll have you. Don't you get everything you ever go after?"

"*What?*"

"Well, look at you. You took all the looks in the family. You're educated. You know how to dress. Women always notice you while I look like the Durham bull in a pea jacket."

Tired as he was, Rob had to laugh. In Dwight's voice, he heard the flip side of his own jealousies.

"I always thought you and Nancy Faye got the family beauty," he grinned. "I sure as hell *knew* who got all the athletic talent."

"And how much good did it do me? You finished college, got a law degree. I'm just an ex-jock and ex-married cop."

"A damn good cop," said Rob. "And you'd have hated law school."

Dwight smiled ruefully and for a moment their faces mirrored each other's. "I know, but every once in a while . . ."

Rob nodded. "Me, too," he confessed.

"Yeah?"

"Yeah."

Her first conscious thought was an awareness of dulled sheets of pain layered upon her body. Then the smell of antiseptics, the blip of electronic monitors, and the sound of moans.

Her moans.

She became aware of a presence beside her and opened her eyes.

The nurse was completely gowned and masked, but her eyes were compassionate. "How do you feel, Mrs. Honeycutt?" she asked gently.

"It hurts," Kate whispered.

The next time she came to, the pain was still with her but somehow more bearable. She lay very still and remembered finding the pictures, realizing that Gordon was actually James, and then lying on the damp dirt floor waiting for death.

She knew she was in a hospital, though, so she was alive, but there was a growing desolation within her as she realized that the baby had not made it. There were no funny little flutters under her heart, no soft little turns and kicks. Only a small weight that lay still and unmoving.

She raised herself on one hip and physical pain shafted through her, but it was nothing compared to what she felt as her unborn infant's body drifted to that side of her womb and she knew that the movement was due to gravity, not independent life.

James had won after all. Jake was completely dead now.

"Mrs. Honeycutt? Mrs. Honeycutt."

Like the nurse earlier, the two doctors were clothed in sterile gowns and masks. "It's Teresa Yates, Mrs. Honeycutt," said the taller figure. "Your obstetrician, remember?"

Kate nodded.

"This is Dr. Yeh, who'll be taking care of you."

Dr. Yeh had chubby cheeks and shiny black eyes that almost disappeared when he smiled at her above his mask. His English was good, but his slight Chinese accent was filtered through Oxford by the sound of it.

"Sorry about the masks, love, but we can't risk bacterial infection. You are quite the lucky young woman," he told Kate. "Your burns are much less extensive than we thought at first. They scrubbed up rather nicely and you shouldn't even have scar tissue. You've lost a lot of fluids, however, and your body's been under enormous stress. We shan't need the heart monitor any longer," he said, removing the leads, "but we'll keep you on IV a few days. Make sure your fluid level gets back to normal. There's a mild anesthetic in it." He rattled off a chemical name that meant nothing to Kate. "It won't take away all the pain, but we can't risk giving you anything that'll cross the placental barrier, can we?"

Kate closed her eyes as involuntary tears spilled down the side of her face.

Dr. Yates took her hand. "What's wrong, Mrs. Honeycutt? The pain too severe?"

"My baby," Kate mourned. "It's dead."

"What?" She quickly fitted the stethoscope to her ears, laid the cool metal disk on Kate's swollen abdomen, and listened intently.

"It doesn't move," Kate cried. "Not since I've been here." And she bit her lips to stop the grief that threatened to spill from the very core of her being.

"Mrs. Honeycutt—Kate, listen," said Dr. Yates. "You've been through an explosion. You've been burned, your whole system has suffered unbelievable stress. And that includes the baby. When I first examined you last night, the baby's heartbeat was arrhythmic and speeded-up. This morning, it's almost back to normal and he's gotten very still. That's completely usual in cases like this. It's as if the body says, 'Okay, cool it, kid.' I promise you that he'll be bouncing around like crazy again in a day or two. In the meantime, here!"

She put the stethoscope to Kate's ears and miraculously the baby's heartbeat was there between her own, like soft spring rain on a tin roof.

They let her go home the day before Easter.

Miss Emily drove Kate's car to pick her up. Lacy came along with his hand still bandaged and Mary Pat had to be cautioned against flinging herself at Kate when they tucked her into the back seat.

"My arms are fine," Kate protested and hugged her little cousin tightly. "We just have to be careful with my legs for another few weeks."

She was slightly disappointed not to see Rob with them. He'd been by the hospital at least once a day since the doctors allowed visitors, and he had sent a flood of flowers, books and silly get-well cards.

"He said there was something he wanted to get for dinner," said Miss Emily. "What he wants, I couldn't tell you. Bessie's cooked one bowl of every food known to civilized mankind."

"Yeah, and how many pies and cakes did you bring over?" Lacy asked her tartly.

"Well, Dwight's coming, too," Miss Emily said, "and he always was a big eater."

"Me, too," said Mary Pat, who seemed to have accepted James's death without any real damage, as if the freedom to voice her misgivings about his identity somehow compensated for his loss.

"Am I really going to come live with you and Uncle Lacy and the baby and Aunt Susie and the kitties?" she asked Kate.

"You are if Rob can arrange it," Kate promised.

It had rained all that week and everything was lushly green. Every stem, blade and leaf was full of water and tender-fresh, and dogwoods and azaleas were at their peak for Easter. Sourweed reddened some fallow fields and toadflax made blue mist of others.

"Willy finished setting his tobacco this week," said Miss Emily when Kate remarked on the fields of young new plants.

"Bluebirds is nesting in every one of my boxes," Lacy reported. "And I heard a chuck-will's-widder two nights ago."

Another season, another beginning, Kate thought, and contentment wrapped her as they drove past Gilead and turned into the lane. She found that she could look at the burned-out shell of the tobacco barn without the deep grief she'd expected.

The inner scars were finally healing.

Rob and Dwight were sitting on the back porch rockers when they drove into the yard, and Bessie immediately appeared at the kitchen door to welcome Kate home and urge everybody to wash up.

"Biscuits'll be out of the stove in ten minutes," she warned, "though where I'll put 'em, I don't know. Won't enough room on that table for an ant to walk sideways and here comes Rob with two more bowls."

"The South's not what it used to be," said Rob with a perfectly straight face. "I found some frozen collards in your freezer, Mother, but I had to try six different grocery stores before I found any chit'lings."

"Chit'lings!" Bessie said disgustedly. "Whoever heard of collard greens and chit'lings at Eastertime?"

"I don't know," Kate said demurely. "They certainly make a change from flowers and candy."

Epilogue

This was where they had spent their wedding night.

His best man had lent them a four-wheel drive and they'd driven it up to Bendo Falls, then backpacked the rest of the way to a high meadow lake near the Canadian border.

That was four children and a second mortgage ago. Her mother had a romantic streak just as wide as theirs, though, and for an anniversary gift, she'd offered to keep the kids so they could go back up to the lake alone.

"Just don't bring me home another grandchild," she'd warned.

The lakeshore was as deserted now as ten years ago and now, as then, the first thing they did was cut hemlock boughs for a mattress, zip their sleeping bags together and make love.

Later, they lay entwined and watched stars come out overhead while loons called across the lake and an owl answered somewhere in the woods behind them.

"I wouldn't mind one more baby," she said. "Would you?"

The curve of her breast echoed the line of mountains beyond the lake. "Another baby would be fine," Will said, thinking how good the years had been and how much he still loved her.

The air was chilly, but all around them spring rustled into being and a flock of late-arriving geese circled the lake with rich melodic honks, then splashed down right in front of them.

"This place is getting too damn crowded," he complained.

She laughed and drew him to her and the smell of her hair was like sunlight on new-mown wheat as they made love again, slower and more tenderly.

Afterwards, he lay flat on his back staring straight up into the blue-black midwestern sky with his hand tangled in her hair. He almost never thought of those nightmarish nights in Vietnam when he'd been a damn-fool kid who thought he could prove he was a man by quitting school and running away to the army, but the cry of the loons reminded him of monkey howls and he found himself remembering the steaming jungles, the smell of gunsmoke and blood, and those guys on that bad patrol when everybody else got killed. There was one with a bushy black beard, and a tall Southerner who'd been kind to him. What was his name? John? Jay?

He felt his wife's soft breaths slow and deepen; and just before sleep claimed him, too, he thought drowsily, "Wonder what ever happened to those guys?"

About the Author

Margaret Maron lives with her artist husband on their family farm near Raleigh, North Carolina. She is a former president of Sisters in Crime.